I0624576

DEATH OF A DENTIST

A Walter Anchor Ghost Detective Story, Case #4

ROBERT J. MCCARTER

Little Hummingbird Publishing

Death of a Dentist

A Walter Anchor Ghost Detective Story

Copyright © 2020 by Robert J. McCarter

Except as permitted under the Copyright Act of 1976, this book may not be reproduced in whole or in part in any manner.

This book is a work of fiction. Names, places, and incidents are either products of the author's imagination or used fictitiously. Any resemblance to actual events or persons, living or dead, is entirely coincidental.

Cover images ©DepositPhoto.com, Buurserstraat38

Version 1.0, May 2020

ISBN: 978-1-941153-39-0

Visit Robert's website at: www.RobertJMcCarter.com

Published by:

Little Hummingbird Publishing

P.O. Box 23518

Flagstaff, AZ 86002

❀ Created with Vellum

Walter Anchor, Ghost Detective Stories

- **Case 1: Detecting Haley** (also part of *Life After: Stories of Life, Death, and the Places in Between*)
- **Case 2: The Ghost Bride's Gift**
- **Case 3: A Long Hard Fall**
- **Case 4: Death of a Dentist**
- **Case 5: A Hollywood Kind of a Murder** (coming July 2020)
- **Case 6: The Red Arrow Murders** (coming September, 2020)
- **Unfinished Business: The Cases of Walter Anchor Ghost Detective** (coming October, 2020)

Prologue

I LOVE EMILY. SHE'S MY BEST FRIEND IN THIS STRANGE earth-bound afterlife. I love her in ways that are obvious and in ways that are not.

I love how she seems to be the most optimistic ghost that I know, channeling the full happiness that you would expect from the four-year-old she looks like. How it can bubble up and just take her over, her cheeks flushing red and her blond Shirly Temple curls bouncing around her round face, the ever-present lollipop on her T-shirt a shining red, communicating her mood to any who cares to look.

And I love the grouchy, world-weary and wise eighty-year-old ghost that Emily is. She was four when she died of dysentery in 1927, and still looks it, but has been dead longer than any of the other ghosts in our Tucson grave-yard. At times her voice will get gravelly, and she will say things that belie her appearance that are either wise or just plain grumpy and sound wise... or sometimes scandalous, saying words a four-year-old shouldn't even know.

I love Emily for saving my afterlife and teaching me

how to be a ghost. For pulling me along like that innocent four-year-old and for shoving me into the things I didn't want to face like that wise old ghost.

But it doesn't mean that I've always liked it. I often haven't. Especially that day.

I was pacing under the washed-out winter Tucson sky, when she came and found me on the roof of the casino. It was a day when my grumpy defenses were operating at full and the plan her old/young self came up with was one I hated.

I didn't want to solve a murder. I didn't want to be a ghost detective. I didn't want to talk to anyone. I wanted to be alone and miserable.

I was pacing the casino roof, on top of the large metal air ducts, mumbling to myself. "You don't need this, Walter. You don't need this."

Below was the home of one of my addictions when I was living. Gambling. For me it was craps and Texas Hold-em. That afternoon, I had flown aimlessly over the sprawl of Tucson and "somehow" ended up there. On that roof. Pacing. Arguing with what was left of that addiction. The thrill of winning. The ache of losing. The escape into something besides my troubles, besides thinking about my past, about how I was murdered and I couldn't crack the case.

When I was alive, I used to do the exact same thing in the parking lot, on the hot asphalt among the cars. My problems were, admittedly, different now, but my actions were the same. Pacing. Mumbling. Trying to resist the lure of senseless escape.

Emily and I had had some tough cases, one recently that dragged me through my past life in Hollywood where I was an actor and married to a beautiful actress. It dragged me through the guilt I felt and forced me to reconcile with my ex-wife, as much as a ghost can. A ghost, that is, with this ghostly typewriter so I could actually communicate with her directly.

I had been fairly content (okay, fairly grumpy) in this strange afterlife trying to find clues to my own murder and stumbling into solving other murders. It was something to do, and it was clearly worth doing. Justice and all of that. But I hadn't wanted to go delving into my past, and when Emily found a bride dead alone in a bridal suite who happened to look very much like my ex-wife, it had let loose that past and sent me examining it, which I hated.

The past should be left in the past.

We had solved some other murders, but because of the case of the Ghost Bride, my past just wouldn't stay where it belonged.

And I think that's what brought me to the casino and the remnants of that old addiction. Something else to lose myself in, and this time I couldn't lose any actual money or put my dental practice at risk.

Yeah. I was a practicing dentist when I died. And yes, before that I had been an actor. And now I'm a ghost and a detective.

Don't ask me. My life and afterlife have taken some strange turns, and it hasn't been boring. But that day, pacing at the casino, I wanted boring. I wanted escape. I wanted anything but what happened.

With a "pop," Emily stood in front of me, her green eyes wide, the lollipop on her T-shirt a bright yellow.

I guess I should explain that shirt. The color of the lollipop was something of a mood ring for the girl, revealing her general mood. Ghosts don't have clothing, per se, but we can, with practice and effort, control our ghostly forms and what we appear to be wearing. In this case, that bright yellow lollipop meant Emily was curious.

So, baby-faced Emily, wide eyed and apparently curious, popped into my pacing path on the roof of that casino.

"Walter," she said, her voice airy, coming out as if she had been running. "Come quick. There's a case you've got to see."

Emily also has a lisp. Completely adorable and combined with her appearance made it hard to remember what an old ghost she was. So that last sentence was way more adorable in Emily-speak: "There'th a cathe you've got to thee."

But adorable wasn't enough for me. I said, "No," rather sharply, turned and paced the other direction.

"Walter! This is important," she said, putting the full force of four-year-old earnestness into the delivery.

Around us was the sprawl of Tucson. Low buildings, only a couple of stories tall at the most, roads and traffic and the endless noise of it. The sky was washed out, dingy with the dust the winds kicked up. To the north were the low craggy hills of Tucson Mountain Park. I might have been fooling myself, but I thought I could hear the comforting dinging of slot machines below us.

"No," I said again, continuing to pace.

I heard another "pop" and Emily was in front of me, her lollipop was edging away from yellow and towards an angry red, her little arms folded over her chest.

"Walter Anthony Anchor!" she yelled, stomping her foot on the duct. She was a ghost, so it didn't make any noise. This ghost happened to be my best friend, so her plea reached me.

I sighed—it was a thing full of resignation and defeat which makes one wonder why Emily kept hanging out with me. I would think that she could do better.

And, no, ghosts don't breathe, although we have a lot of flesh-and-blood habits left over with analogous effect.

"What is the case?" I asked.

Emily's green eyes lit up and she rushed up to me and took my arm. "Let me show you."

EMILY ALWAYS TANTALIZED ME WITH THE DETAILS OF A case. Usually something lurid. Like, "A true crime of passion, you've got to see this," or "The bum is smushed like a bug," or "This is a gruesome one, bub."

But not this time. She took my slightest agreement, grabbed my arm, and popped me to the scene of the crime.

"Popping" is what we call it when a ghost goes from one place to another, instantaneously. It has that name because of the sound it makes when the ghost leaves or appears. Not all ghosts can pop. Emily is very good at it. I've only managed it a couple of times in extreme situations. This means that it can be very difficult for me to get away from Emily if she's determined. Popping, for a ghost like Emily, extends to people as well as places.

The room we popped to was one I instantly recognized. How could I not? It was one of the treatment rooms of my former dental practice. It had been painted, obliterating the gorgeous mural I had on one wall. A picture of Marilyn Monroe from *The Seven Year Itch*, the one where she's in heels and a white dress standing on a grate in New York City, wind blowing the skirt up around her, a dazzling smile on her face. An iconic image that went with the name of my practice, "Hollywood Dental," and showed off Ms. Monroe's excellent teeth.

Before going to dental school, I made a go of being an

actor. Sarah Michele Gellar once vanquished me on *Buffy the Vampire Slayer,* and as a cowboy, I once died in the arms of Jane Seymour's *Dr. Quinn, Medicine Woman.* Those were my acting claims to fame, but I mostly worked as a grip in Hollywood and paid for dental school that way.

And I fell in love with an actress whose name you would recognize, married her, got divorced, and ran away from Hollywood back to my hometown, Tucson, Arizona. That "Hollywood Dental" on the door was my marketing ploy and an homage to the life I wished I had.

Yeah, I don't always make things easy on myself.

"Emily..." I began, confused.

This was the room where I died. The room where I "woke up" dead with a needle in my arm. This is the room where the world thought I died of a self-administered propofol overdose.

She had a guilty look on her round face and her lollipop had gone a dull yellow with swirls of red. She was worried and guilty, maybe a little bit angry. I had never seen the lollipop look like this, meaning that these were complicated emotions.

"What are we doing here?" I asked. I didn't have a mood-ring style tell on my ghostly form, but if I did it would also be a swirl of colors. Red for angry. Yellow for confused. Black for the dark mood that was creeping up the back of my neck.

As it was, I had on a trench coat and a fedora looking like a 1940's detective—Emily's idea—which would have fit in nicely with the picture of Monroe from 1954.

Her bottom lip quivered and she wouldn't meet my gaze.

"Emily!" I shouted and immediately regretted it as she jumped back like a scared animal. I squatted down to get to her level. "Honey. My case is cold. What are we doing here?"

She pursed her lips and her jaw set. "We need to solve your case," she said slowly. "So we are going to start over."

Emily had been directive with me. Sometimes very. Especially when I was a new ghost and didn't know anything. But she had never been this way about my own death.

I searched for the words. Something that would say that this was not only useless, this would probably be very bad for me. Seeing Sun, my ex-wife, had been as horrible as it was wonderful. It reminded me of what I had lost and now that I was dead, I could never have what I had wanted the most.

Hollywood Dental had kind of been my consolation prize. My way to make it in this world that wasn't acting and wasn't with Sun. I had trouble with gambling. And, yes, I had trouble with propofol making the whole "he overdosed" thing easy to believe. But I had gotten past my addictions. I had started to do better. My last day alive was an ordinary day at the office.

"No," I said, crossing my arms and mirroring her stance.

"Yes, we are," she said, her nose scrunching up comically in her seriousness.

"No, we are not," I said.

Let me tell you this, from long experience with Emily. Don't try to out four-year-old a four-year-old. Even one that's been dead for over eighty years. You can't. It won't work.

But I tried. The standoff continued for several minutes. I flew up to the roof and she popped me back to the room. I walked through the wall to the outside of the bland office building and she popped me back to the room. I yelled.

7

She yelled. It was childish and silly and she was not giving up.

"Why, Emily?" I finally asked, staring at the stupid mauve wall that used to have a classic Hollywood image on it. I was avoiding looking at the dental chair, where I died, and was fixated on how my partner had thrown away what was special about Hollywood Dental when he changed the name and painted the walls. "Why now? What good will it do?"

Emily let out a long sigh. "I miss you, Walter," she said quietly, her arms relaxing as she stared at her bare feet. "I miss when cases were fun, when you listened to me, when we were…"

She looked up and there were tears running down her cheek.

It was the pure unadulterated grief of a four-year-old. Big crocodile tears, quivery lip, runny nose, rosy cheeks.

"When we were what, Emily?" I asked. I had to know. That look dragged the words out of me. I was so stupid.

"When we were partners," she said with a sniff.

AND THERE IT IS. THE POWER OF EMILY TO LAY ME OUT emotionally. It's like this was a boxing match and that was the moment where the bell rings, the referee raises Emily's gloved hand into the air and shouts, "We have a winner by a knockout!"

Sun was the partner I had wanted. And she had been. We had been married. We were both struggling actors together. She got pregnant. And one rainy day on the LA freeways, an accident caused a miscarriage, and that was something our marriage could not recover from.

Emily wasn't my partner like that, not in a romantic

sense—and, yes, there are those kinds of relationships among ghosts, although it's not quite what you think—but we were partners. We spent significant time together. We solved murders. We brought people to justice. We shared a path and a purpose.

It wasn't the partnership I had wanted (that would be my beautiful Sun), but it was the partnership I needed. And despite my often foul mood, it was one I cherished.

My mouth moved as I struggled to speak and I let my gaze wander around the room. A counter with a sink and faux wood cabinets with a monitor and keyboard sitting on it. The blue dental chair with the long arm of the light hanging from the ceiling. A chair and a stool.

It was a small room, but one so familiar, the painting over of the mural the only change from when it had been mine.

I let myself look at the room, all of the room, and I tried not to bolt.

I hadn't been back here. I had told Emily about it, but I hadn't been in the room, and that brought with it a rush of memories. I felt my ghostly form changing and looked down and saw that I was wearing blue scrubs which I had spent so many years in.

This is my default ghostly form, the one I first had before taking on the 1940's detective look for Emily. It was how I looked in this office every day for five years. I felt vulnerable looking this way again, as if that trench coat and fedora had become armor for me, a shield against my past, and now that it was gone, I couldn't keep the past at bay anymore.

I looked at Emily's green eyes and there was compassion there but also a hardness. A dedication to this path she had dragged me on to.

"What do you want?" I asked.

She smiled, it was tentative and shy. Her brow furrowed and she licked her lips.

"There's something here," she said slowly. "Something we missed. I know it. I want you to walk me through your day, your last day here. Everything. One step at a time. Leave nothing out."

If I had had a body I would have been shaking. I would rather do anything but this. But Emily. For my partner. For my best friend.

I swallowed hard and nodded. Now that I was in scrubs, now that I was here, I knew it would be easy and so very hard. Easy to remember but so hard to relive it all.

I walked out of the former Monroe room and into the small reception area and nodded to the curved Formica counter and the computer sitting on the desk behind it.

"My day... my last day, started here," I said. "I was in early. I was on Yelp, looking at my reviews."

She raised her right eyebrow and gave me an encouraging nod.

The details came flooding back and I told her everything.

Well... almost everything.

Part One

LIVING

Chapter One

BEING A DENTIST IS NOT ALL THE GLAMOUR OF WIELDING a drill, hollowing out decayed parts of teeth while keeping your patient calm, and then stuffing in synthetic substances. Oh no.

And it's not all the fun of delicate injections into the gums or fitting crowns or root planning.

And yes, ladies and gentlemen, those *are* the fun parts. Perhaps now you know why the suicide rate for dentists is so high. And even though my death looked like a suicide, and I knew of no one in this world that wanted me dead— well, maybe a few patients who didn't have an optimal experience—it was most definitely *not* a suicide.

Much of a dental practice is accounting, marketing, and being your own HR department. That morning, my last morning as a living human being, I had gotten in early and looked at the books and then wandered the office. From the curved blue Formica of the reception area with the simple, comfortable armchairs in light pastel shades, to the three treatment rooms, each one with a mural on one of the walls. The Monroe room. The Casablanca room. And the Mary Poppins room for the kids.

I straightened up the magazines in the waiting area and ended up behind the reception desk on the computer looking at Yelp for new ratings and to ritualistically beat myself up about the one-star ratings:

"Has no personality, like a dead fish except smells worse."

"Talks too much. I don't care that the loser was on TV."

"Hit a nerve with that damn needle and I passed out and woke up in the ER. Thanks, Dr. Anchor, you almost sunk my ship."

My name is Walter Anchor, so I found the "sunk my ship" slight particularly galling. And that morning, there was a new 5-star rating that did catch my attention:

"I can't stand dentists or the drill, but Doc Anchor and his magic propofol made it all right!"

I smiled, because that's why I started with the propofol —to help patients. It's a bit of a tricky drug, though, a strong anesthetic and the dosages are hard to get right. But then I felt that smile turn into something that wasn't happiness at a job well done but longing for something that wasn't good for me.

I wanted to numb the pain. I wanted to have that brief high where you know there are issues, there are problems, but you just don't care anymore.

"Good morning, Walter," Midge, my office manager, said, a smile on her round Midwesterner's face, a frilly black sweater on over her scrubs that emphasized how her shoulder-length brown hair was starting to be invaded by grey.

I looked up, trying to wipe that embarrassing smile off my face, my eyes roaming towards the supply room and the locked cabinet that contained the glass vials of milky-white substance that I so wanted right then. The cabinet that I didn't have the key for, but Midge did.

"Everything all right, hon?" she asked, coming back behind the reception desk, her brow furrowed and her lips pursed in a most motherly fashion, her foofy perfume flowing after her like a cloud. At forty-one, I'm only about ten years younger than Midge, but she's a mother through and through, and the mother of this office.

My eyes refused to meet hers and I pointed lamely at the screen. "Just torturing myself with Yelp," I said with a shrug.

She smiled, one of those motherly smiles of pity, and shook her head. "Enough of that. Now shoo. Doctor Wheeler will be here any moment and you don't want him to see you moping. I'll get the coffee going, looks like you could use some, hon."

DOCTOR ELIAS WHEELER. MY YOUNGER, HANDSOMER, fitter practice mate. He had an endless parade of lovely women by his side and a thousand-watt smile. With his shaved head and his true salesman's heart, I brought him onboard three years earlier because he was the kind of guy that could sell heaters in Tucson in the summer. Of all the "not fun" parts of running this business, getting new clients in was the worst for me, and Doctor Wheeler loved it—a lot more than the drilling—and that just made him a weirdo to me.

Suffice to say that I needed Doctor Wheeler, but I didn't particularly like him. Midge said just the right thing. I definitely did not want him to see me moping.

So I got up and went into the supply room... because

that's what I do in the morning. Look at the schedule and make sure we have all we need for the procedures. And yes, I have staff to do that, but it was always a habit of mine to double-check. Not a good idea to get halfway through a procedure and find you don't have what you need to finish it. "Oh… sorry, Mrs. Evenington, but we're out of the material we create temporary crowns with. You'll have to survive for a day with that sharp stub of a tooth." Yeah, that will get you a big, fat one-star on Yelp.

But this morning, I went in there and stared at the locked steel-grey cabinet. The one with the enticing vials of milky-white liquid. The propofol. It was just a short metal cabinet with a cheap lock. It would take three seconds with a screwdriver to open it up, but it was the lock and the shame of everyone knowing that kept me from doing that.

Well, to be precise, the shame of Mother Midge seeing that cabinet and knowing what I had done was shame enough to stop me. She had found me, more than once, when she came in to open the office, passed out in a dental chair from a propofol session.

The cabinet was the compromise that got her to stay on the job. I had wanted to brush it off, she had wanted to get all the propofol out of the office. The cabinet was detente.

Right above the cabinet was a picture of my ex-wife Sun and me on the set of a movie she was acting in and I was working on as a grip. Behind us are some rolling California hills and Sun has her sunglasses on, her long black hair framing the smile on her beautiful face. She's got her arm around me and is flashing a big thumbs-up.

We're about three months married and this minor part in this major movie has made Sun very happy. We are both very happy, the honeymoon period still full in force.

My curly black hair is disheveled (kind of like always) and I look so damn happy. Like nothing could ever change, that we would always be that happy, be that hopeful, be that in love.

I put that picture there above that locked cabinet for a reason. And yes, it's a bit like Yelp in that it can be a form of self-torture, but I wanted an extra layer on top of the cheap lock and the promise I made to Midge. It's there to remind me of better times and a better me that didn't need the damn propofol (or poker for that matter) to be all right.

Except I wasn't all right.

"Good morning, Hollywood Dental," I heard Doctor Wheeler call. It was his usual, overly cheerful greeting when he came into the office every morning.

I groaned. I wasn't fond of the man.

"Good morning, Walter," Doctor Wheeler said with a jaunty nod a moment later as he strode into the room.

I turned away from the picture and went to the coffeepot and poured myself a cup. Hollywood Dental was not a big office, so the one room housed supplies and had a small fridge and coffeepot and served as the break room.

"Good morning, Doctor Wheeler," I said, trying to put a genuine smile on my face and ignoring for the thousandth time that he called me "Walter" and I called him "Doctor Wheeler." We were colleagues, yes, but not friends, not in the least, and he hadn't earned the right to call me by my first name.

He rubbed at his "Mr. Clean" shaved head in a gesture that made me wonder if he missed his hair. I ruffled my abundant curls, just to emphasize my thick hair.

"I've got two crowns coming in today and a root canal," he began as he put too much sugar into his coffee. "You?"

This was his game. I had brought him on because he

was good at sales, good at bringing in new patients, but he had a habit of rubbing it in.

Well, that day, I still considered that perhaps this was his egotistical way of making sure that I knew he was pulling his load—I was the boss, after all. Now, though, I know different. He just liked to rub my nose in the fact that he was doing more of the expensive procedures than I was.

"Oh, you know," I replied slowly as I took a noisy sip of coffee. "Saving the world one mouth at a time."

His brow furrowed, quite the show with his shaved head, the wrinkles rippling up past where his hairline should have been. And then he smiled, his teeth bleached so white they could almost blind you. "I like that, Walter. 'Saving the world one mouth at a time.' You know, maybe that should be our new motto. 'Hollywood Dental: Saving the World One Mouth at a Time.'" He said it like he was a radio announcer from the fifties.

He chuckled and clapped me on the back on his way out. I couldn't tell if he was making fun of me or not.

It might have been my last day living, but I didn't know that yet. It was just the start of another day at the office.

Chapter Two

I STARED AT EMILY FROM THE STOREROOM/BREAK ROOM of my former dental office. I had paced around the empty office and told her the story of my last day going to each place I spoke of, feeling the feelings, almost seeing what had happened.

"It was just another day," I said with a weak shrug, still getting used to my ghostly form being in scrubs again.

Her lollipop was yellow, both dull and bright swirling together. I think she was both worried and curious.

The storeroom still had a metal cabinet in it, although it was black instead of the dull grey it had been on that day, but the picture of Sun and me still hung above it.

Doctor Wheeler hadn't taken it down when he had transformed Hollywood Dental into Wheeler Dental, when he transformed it from a practice with personality to a generic dental practice.

"It's a nice picture," Emily said. "You look happy."

I nodded. "I was. We had no money and I had already shifted away from acting and was doing grip work to put myself through school. But Sun was starting to get gigs and her happiness was contagious."

"Kinda surprised that your bald compatriot didn't take it down," she said.

I shrugged. "He would have. He took down all of my Hollywood pictures that were hanging in the lobby, but Midge is still working here and Midge insisted."

"Sounds like that broad has some moxy," Emily said, slipping into 1920s speak. Slang can be strange with her. She's seen the language evolve over the decades and has picked up pieces of it here and there.

I smiled. "That she does. Mother Midge can be a force to be reckoned with." The smile evaporated as my mind traveled forward to after I had died, to when I was haunting the practice.

I looked at Emily. "Maybe we should skip ahead. Things are more interesting after I died."

She shook her head, her tight, blond curls bouncing around her young face. "One step at a time, bub. I want to hear it all."

I nodded. There was logic there. I had told Emily all about my last day, but being here, the memories were richer, they were right there at the edge of my consciousness like they wanted to come out.

But this wasn't a good feeling. It was like there was something in there that I didn't want to know. Something that would change how I lived my afterlife.

Chapter Three

HALEY CALCO HAD LONG BROWN HAIR, PALE BLUE EYES, and a shy smile. She was slim like many of the young ones are, her blue scrubs hanging off her a bit too loosely.

It was that last day, my death day, and we were in the Monroe room, the picture of Marilyn looking on as we worked. As I drilled into Mrs. Champon's mouth, I caught Haley staring at me several times, instead of watching the action.

She was new, substituting for Mary Paulson who was on maternity leave, and Haley had a crush on me.

At least I think she did.

And while I didn't really mind the attention, I was far too old for her. And while I used to be an actor, I am, by no means, Hollywood handsome. I'm just plain everyday handsome. My acting career, while I was still thinking of it as a "career," was headed strongly into character actor territory, not leading man. Sun, now she was Hollywood beautiful, and far out of my league, but her beauty has served her well in Hollywood.

Back behind the front desk there were a few of my

Hollywood pictures hanging. When I interviewed Haley for the temp position and she had the opportunity to ask me questions, she said, "So you know Sarah Michelle Gellar?"

I suppressed a smile and said, "We worked together for a couple of days. I can't say that I 'know' her."

"But Sarah Michelle Gellar. Buffy. That must have been…"

And then I had to smile. Haley was young and ideal-istic and somehow thought just because Sarah was famous, she didn't have the same human hang-ups and problems as the rest of us. Fame brings with it a host of opportunities for the enhancement of our human foibles.

"She was very nice," I said, because it felt like I needed to say something.

The memory would often resurface when I caught Haley staring at me. Part of what she was feeling had to do with the life I had briefly lived that looks to the world to be very glamorous, but most of the time is far from it.

"Suction," I said, releasing the trigger on the drill. "Almost there, Mrs. Champon. You're doing great."

The whole Hollywood thing I had going on here was, in part, a marketing ploy. Look, there I am with Sarah Michelle Gellar. Look, there I am with Jane Seymour, and here I am with Johnny Depp (just ignore the fact that my small part was cut out of the final film). I wasn't an overt salesman like Doctor Wheeler, but it helped patients feel comfortable with me. And, in some cases, it contributed to how some of my employees felt about me.

And as ashamed as I was of my failed marriage, of giving up on my dream and running back to Arizona to drill in people's teeth, I didn't want to forget the Holly-wood days.

Yup. It's a bit like the Yelp ratings I was obsessed with. It could be torture, but it was a part of myself I wasn't willing to let go of. The bits of glamour that I did experience, the awe I felt at rubbing elbows with famous people. I was still drawn to it, still wanted it. And it was never going to happen.

"That's good," I said to Haley, and got back to drilling.

She nodded, pulled the suction tube out of Mrs. Champon's mouth, and didn't say anything. She acted shy, this Haley, but I could see a spark in her eyes from time to time. There was something there that made me curious.

And truth was, I was a lonely man. I had given up gambling, had locked away the propofol, but what else did I have besides this practice and Gambler's Anonymous meetings?

There. Haley was staring at me again and I had to smile underneath my mask. I shouldn't like the attention, but I did.

Chapter Four

"THAT HALEY?" EMILY ASKED HER EYEBROW ARCHED and her lips pursed.

"Yes," I said with a sigh. This time I was staring at the chair I had died in in the now bland treatment room. This had been my room, the room I worked in, the room that was my home for so many years. "Haley who we discovered murdered following the one lead we had in my case," I said. "Haley who I had pretended to like to keep her from losing herself to the bardo."

The bardo. Where do I start with that? Our community of ghosts, like any other, has words that are shortcuts to much bigger concepts. The bardo is the place those cliched slack-jawed ghosts are in. It's basically a hell of their own making where they are reliving their regrets. It's where I would have ended up without Emily.

This is the place Emily saved me from when she found me. And this is the place I saved Haley from by distracting her, pretending I had a thing for her.

"Well this explains a lot," Emily said, nodding her head, her curls bouncing around her face.

And it does. I had fallen for Haley when I "pretended" that I liked her, when we were both dead and age didn't matter, when I wanted to believe I was still attractive to the opposite sex even though I didn't have a body anymore.

I've already written about the train wreck that all turned into and won't be dragging that up further. Suffice it to say we were deep into a very uncomfortable part of my past.

"You liked her," Emily continued.

I shrugged again. "I guess. I mean, it felt weird because I was just about old enough to be her father, so I didn't let myself feel much of anything."

"But you liked her," Emily continued with a smile, acting the age she looked. "You were all googly-eyed thinking how pretty she was."

"Yes and no," I said, crossing my arms. "She was pretty, sure, but she wasn't Sun. She was too young. I was lonely."

She squinted her eyes and it seemed like she was looking into me, not at me, using her formidable ghostly intuition—all of us are more intuitive dead, but some more than others. She nodded slowly, apparently satisfied. "So you liked her," she said with a wicked smile, now more the eighty-year-old ghost.

"Yes, Emily," I said, sighing yet again. There was clearly going to be a lot of sighing going through my past at this resolution. "I liked her."

Emily nodded, a smile on her face. Clearly, she was enjoying this a lot more than me.

Chapter Five

AT THE END OF MY LAST DAY AS A CORPOREAL BEING, Haley Calco was there in front of the reception desk dressed in jeans and a silky blue blouse that went well with her eyes.

I was tired, still dressed in my ever-present scrubs having just finished a root canal that almost went bad. I wanted a drink... no, what I wanted was a good card game, or better yet, a nice propofol session.

"Haley?" I asked. "Why are you still here?"

She smiled shyly looking down at her sandals. I had close to twenty years on her, and in this moment it showed. I looked around and the office was empty, the light filtering in the waiting room window a dusky orange.

"Well... I..." she stammered, her pale blue eyes briefly meeting mine before they wandered to the photo of my *Buffy the Vampire Slayer* episode.

My heart thudded in my chest and I felt like a teenager, much younger than the twenty-something Haley. She wasn't going to ask me out, was she? That would be so very inappropriate, but my lonely heart not-so-secretly hoped she would.

The sound of my breathing was way too loud and I tried putting my hands in the pockets of my scrubs so I could look relaxed, but the pockets weren't very deep and I just ended up looking dorky. I could smell her sweet perfume, and while she was not my type—my Korean American ex-wife Sun was my type—the loneliness and isolation of this life had made me desperate.

I'm not proud to say it. But if I'm going to look at my past this myopically, if I'm going to find my murderer, I need to be honest with myself.

She bit her lip and took a deep breath, her red lips parting—had she just put on lipstick? She had. Oh boy. Here it comes.

"So... Doctor Anchor..." she began.

"Yes, Haley? You can tell me anything, you know that, right?" That was a phrase straight out of the HR side of my job, but true enough.

She nodded and bit her lip again. "I was... I am..." She took a deep breath and squared her shoulders. "I am hoping that after Mary returns from maternity leave that there will still be a place for me here at Hollywood Dental."

She ended with a bright smile and my heart sank because this wasn't about her being attracted to me. This wasn't me finding out that women can still be attracted to me. Those glances earlier were about this. She was sizing me up. Figuring out what to say. Those words, once they came out, sounded decidedly practiced.

But I am an actor... or, at least, I used to be one. I put a bright smile on my face and said, "I hope we can work that out, Haley. We'll just have to see."

She nodded shyly and we exchanged a few pleasantries, but she got out of there quickly.

I didn't know it then, but it was the last time I would see Haley alive and the last time Haley would see me alive, but it wasn't the last time we would see each other.

After she left, the shame I had held back came flooding in, my cheeks burning hot. I marched into the supply room and stared at the steel-grey cabinet that held the propofol, wondering if I took it quickly enough if it would erase the memory of what had just happened.

I was just about old enough to be Haley's father. Of course, she was not interested in me. How stupid was I? If I wanted to date, I needed to get on one of those websites, but I just couldn't.

My eyes wandered up to the photo of Sun and me, so happy. What I wanted was Sun, and I could never have her.

I turned, walked out and slumped down into the chair behind the counter. No propofol. I was past that. No gambling. My financial life could not take it. And while my life was nothing great, I did have this practice and I wanted to keep it.

I tried to dig into the charting I had left to do, but I just didn't have the focus for it. I wiggled the mouse and went to Yelp. At least there was one unhealthy thing I wouldn't feel too guilty about doing.

AFTER HALEY LEFT, MOTHER MIDGE WANDERED IN AND saw me slumped behind the desk staring at Yelp, the one-star reviews sorted to the top. My face was slack and I kept looking at the door Haley had walked through.

I was feeling old and rather sorry for myself. Haley

hadn't been interested in me, just interested in keeping her job. Well... that's not true. She was interested in me in so far as I was the source of her job.

"You okay there, Walter?" Midge asked, her voice taking on that gentle "I'm worried you are going to use again" tone.

I turned, put on a smile, and nodded. "Of course. Haley was just pitching to keep her job after Mary comes back."

Midge cocked her head and looked closely at me. She knew when I was acting, and I had just been acting.

"She can be a handful," Midge said, an eyebrow arching. "She looks all pretty and young and innocent, but that girl has got a temper on her. Let me tell you."

I nodded absently. I hadn't seen it, but I believed it. There was something dangerous in those blue eyes of hers.

"But..." Midge continued, "we could probably work it out. She is good with the patients."

Now I was the one giving Midge the look. I expected her to tell me that when Mary was back from maternity leave we wouldn't need her, that I would have to let her go. "Really?"

Midge nodded cheerfully but wouldn't meet my eyes. Something was going on.

"I've got to get home, hon," she said, a slight blush of red invading her round cheeks. "Hal will gnaw his own foot off if I don't get him something to eat."

"Okay, Midge. Thanks for everything today." I knew there was something to get to the bottom of, but I just didn't have the energy.

She stopped at the door and turned back, her eyes finally meeting mine. "Go home, Walter. Get some rest." What she was really saying was, "Don't use, Walter."

I nodded my head and lied, "I'll do that."

After she was gone, all thoughts of self-torture via Yelp left me and I wandered through the office trying to figure it out. What were Midge and Haley up to? Why did Midge want to keep her around?

The two of them, they were keeping something from me.

It was a mystery and I was no detective. I was alone in my offices having no one to question. I could only move around, look around, and think about it.

Writing this, it was a strange prescient moment that outlined what my life—rather, afterlife—would soon be.

And that mystery, what Haley and Midge were up to, is a mystery I have solved, but not until after I was dead. I won't go into the details here but suffice to say that it was a twisty little mystery that involved Haley's murder and a bit of a smuggling operation going on in my office.

But it was a dead-end as to my own murder. I was ignorant of it when I was alive and wasn't a threat to the scheme because of that ignorance. There was no reason to kill me.

Back in the office, that night, my last night as a biological being, I walked and I searched through desks and filing cabinets and I worried until well after midnight.

I was tired, punch-drunk tired, but the mystery had derailed me from my trip to shame town, so using wasn't even on my mind.

I remember being frustrated and exhausted. I turned off the office lights and stumbled into the Monroe room and got into the dental chair. I needed a few minutes of rest before going home.

I lay down, took a deep breath in the darkness, enjoying the antiseptic tang in the air, and immediately fell asleep.

Chapter Six

I sat on the floor of the former Monroe room staring at the bland industrial carpet. It was vaguely blue, but up close there were enough colors in there that I wouldn't have called it blue. It had grey and off-white and teal, but nothing that was straight-up blue.

It's interesting that I always thought of it as blue, that I never looked close enough to see the constituent parts. That I had never understood the illusion of my carpet.

"I'm sorry, Walter," Emily said gently. She was sitting beside me staring at me, not the carpet. "That must have been a tough moment with Haley."

I have to wonder if she was starting to see the strands that made up me, the pieces of my last day. That maybe if she knew enough of my pieces that the illusion would dissolve and I wouldn't be who she thought I was. That she wouldn't want to spend time with me anymore.

I tried to smile, but I'm sure it came out all twisted and weird. I was too in it to pretend that it wasn't a bad moment. It was, but it was just a moment. Just a brief moment of shame on the long road of my life.

Try being an actor and going to endless auditions and being constantly rejected. This wasn't that big of a deal in the scheme of things.

"What is it, Walter?" Emily asked, putting her hand on my shoulder and doing it right so I felt that ghostly sense of touch, that barely there sensation. It's not like when you are alive, but touch is still important even when you aren't physical.

I sighed. "I…" I began, but looked away.

"What?" Emily asked.

"You know how we have such good memories?" I asked.

Emily nodded, her green eyes wide as she stared at me.

"Well… doing this. Being here. Telling it all to you…"

Her face melted into a compassionate smile. "You are remembering more things," she offered.

I nodded. "Things I hadn't wanted to remember," I said.

"Worse than Haley?" she asked.

"Much worse."

Chapter Seven

My phone rang, drilling into my brain like a nervous dentist in training. I didn't know where I was. The phone was buzzing against my chest and I reached into the pocket of my scrubs and pulled it out.

It said "Sun."

My heart thudded in my chest and I was suddenly sweating. I looked around in the dim light of nighttime Tucson shining in through the window and felt the faux leather underneath me and knew I had fallen asleep in the office. Again.

I briefly remembered the shame at thinking Haley had been attracted to me, that I had then wondered why Midge wanted to keep Haley and ended up searching the office late into the night, finally coming into the Monroe room to lie down for a few minutes on the dental chair before going home.

But it was Sun calling. It had been close to two years since we had talked. We were down to Christmas cards and the rare email. And the hour... It was almost 1:30 a.m. Something had to be wrong.

I sat up, flicked the screen to answer, and put the phone to my ear. "Sun? Is everything okay?"

"Hi, Walter," she said, her voice slightly slurred. She had been drinking. "It's good to hear your voice."

I blinked and nodded. She must be drunk if she was saying that. My heart beat harder. "It's good to hear your voice too, Sun. So… what's going on?"

"You were awake, right?" she asked, some surprise in her voice as if she had just realized the time. "I didn't wake you, did I?"

"No," I lied. "I'm still at the office. Catching up on paperwork."

She barked out a laugh. "Hard to imagine my Walter buried in paperwork and not carrying half his weight in gear rushing from setup to setup."

After the acting petered out, I worked as a grip and funded my dental training. I worked on Sun's first big commercial—it was how we met.

"Do you miss it?" she asked. And then I knew she was more than a little drunk. We never talked about my old life.

"Of course, Sun. I miss it. I miss—" I cut myself off. I was going to say, "I miss you," but she wasn't drunk enough for that. There was no drunk enough for that.

Sun and I had taken our shot and the accident and then our miscarriage had been the thing we couldn't get over. The thing that took us out. The thing you couldn't plan for or defend against. A goddamn accident that cost me what I cared about the most. Her pregnancy was a promise of our future together and after that accident, after we lost our child, that future was unobtainable.

"I miss you too, Walter," she whispered. "I do. I swear I do. But… You know…"

I nodded. We had been over this. Looking at me reminded her of the child we lost, of the life we almost had. "I know," I said. "It was just bad luck. A terrible day."

Sun sniffed loudly. Was she crying now? My heart, which had calmed down a bit, kicked back into high gear. What was going on?

"So, listen, Walter. I... I need to warn you about something."

"Warn me...?" I asked, the small room suddenly making me feel claustrophobic.

"The paparazzi, they... pictures, you know... probably on the internet already." She ended in a sigh. "I don't even know if it's going anywhere, but he's famous and..."

She wasn't being very clear, but the picture clicked into place. Sun had been photographed on a date and it was about to be tabloid fodder and all over social media.

I was never successful enough for anyone to take pictures of me and neither was Sun when we were together. This was one aspect of my failure as an actor that I was okay with. I never wanted to be famous, which may sound weird for an actor. I got off on the process, on the art, fame was a side effect, from my point of view, and not a desirable one.

My heart beat harder and I was sweating. I didn't want to see Sun glammed up and out with a Hollywood-hand-some hunk. I didn't want to think about what my "not quite over Sun" brain would imagine. It had been years now, but Sun was still the love of my life. There wasn't really a time when I didn't want her back.

But I swallowed all of that because she *was* the love of my life and I wanted her to be happy.

"Is he good to you?" I asked quietly.

She sniffed again. "Yeah. He's... he's kind and thoughtful. Surprisingly so."

"Then don't worry about it, Sun," I said, forcing a

smile on my face that she couldn't see. "Focus on your life and forget about all that crap."

"But... I just didn't want you to be surprised. I... I worry about you, Walter."

And she had reason to. I had to borrow money from her to dig out of my gambling problem and she knew about my dance with propofol. I can't say we were close, but I kept tabs on her as she did on me.

"I'm fine," I lied. It had been a bad day with that Haley stupidity, the mystery I couldn't solve, and this was just making it worse. My background longing for propofol was quickly edging towards need. "Really. I'm glad you told me, Sun. I really do appreciate it."

"Yeah?" she asked.

"Yeah," I said, putting some punch in my voice that I wasn't feeling. "I am always happy to talk to my favorite actress. Quite the honor, really. I am your biggest fan."

"Shut up, Walter," she said.

"No, Sun. You are my favorite. By far. I snagged one of your season five posters. The one with you out front and center and the other four behind you in front of the LA skyline. 'Detectives: LA coming fall of 2010.'"

She groaned. "Yeah, I call that one the 'butt shot.' The men can face the camera head on, but the girls have to twist to the side and show their asses."

"Yeah. That one," I said. "It's why I like it so much."

"I bet." She chuckled but went silent for a few breaths. "Seriously, Walter. Are you okay with this? I do worry about you. You're a goddamn dentist. You could have stayed in Hollywood. You'd probably be directing by now."

Sun never understood the whole dentist thing. I mean, she must have intellectually. I promised my father that if I didn't make it in Hollywood after ten years, I would go get myself educated, find a career. But she had the drive it took to make it in Hollywood and I didn't. If you couldn't be an actor, being a grip wasn't a bad way to go, but watching actors all day and not being one was just too hard.

"I'm good. I really am," I said. "I have an annoying partner and the HR stuff drives me mad, but every day I get to use my acting skills to ease nervous patients and help them. It's a good life, Sun. I chose this life." It sounded like I meant it, and most of me did.

"Okay, okay," she said with a tiny chuckle. "You are clearly more emotionally mature than me. Because I would be a whiney baby if I couldn't spend my days acting."

"Oh, Sun, I act each and every day," I said with a chuckle. "I act like the calmest dentist on the planet. I act like a businessman who knows what he is doing." And sometimes I act like the person my ex-wife needs me to be, but I didn't say that part.

She laughed and it was a beautiful sound, a happy sound. It had been a very long time since I had made her laugh.

I lay back down in the chair and we talked for another twenty minutes, mostly her delivering day-to-day minutia about her life as a lead on a major network TV show.

I loved hearing about it and I was so happy for her, but I was sad for me. But I am a good enough actor and she had had enough to drink that she didn't notice.

After she hung up, I closed my eyes, squeezed them shut and didn't dare move. If I got up, I would head towards that grey cabinet and the propofol locked inside. If I searched for Sun on my phone and saw her with the Hollywood hunk she was seeing, I would rip my hair out and then go for the propofol.

And I wasn't going to go for the propofol.

I was not.

I made a decision then as the moments ticked by with excruciating slowness. No more propofol in the office. It was useful. It helped some patients. But this was my practice and I wasn't safe with it.

At least something good had come of this crappy day.

I took it one breath at a time until I fell asleep.

I have no memory of waking up until I was a ghost looking at my own dead body.

Chapter Eight

"WHAT IF I WASN'T MURDERED?" I ASKED EMILY. I spoke the words slowly, carefully, as if I were still corporeal and my mouth was filled with glass.

We were still sitting on the floor of what used to be the Monroe room, on that carpet that looked blue but was made up of all those other colors.

The room felt empty, too quiet. Outside the sun was setting, and while I could hear the rumble of the road, it felt distant. It felt like Emily and I were isolated and alone. I mean, we were. It was Saturday and no one was in the office, but more than that. Like this here, this story and her were my entire world.

Emily blinked, her green eyes wide. Her mouth moved and she fidgeted with her fingers. If any ghost knows how important being murdered is to me, it's Emily.

And I know that may sound strange, but think about it. If someone murdered me, then I have a mission as a ghost, something to do, unfinished business that points outward at my murderer. Then all this running around with Emily solving murders makes sense.

If I was an addict that slipped after a very bad day and overdosed, then not only was my life a mess, but my after-life no longer has meaning.

And living or dead, to have any sort of balance, you have to have meaning.

Emily's smooth brow furrowed, her mouth moved, and her eyes flicked away from me and I knew she had figured it all out.

"You were murdered," she said, standing up and straightening her shoulders. "You know me, Walter, I can smell a murder. And you were murdered."

It was sweet of her, it really was, but I didn't believe it.

"But if I am really a detective now..." I began. "If *we* are really detectives now, don't we have to look at the cold hard facts? Shouldn't we apply Occam's razor?"

Her lips pressed into a thin line. "Of course."

I shrugged weakly. "My last day wasn't a good one," I said. "That Haley thing was bad enough but... Sun. My Sun had called me after two years to tell me about the famous man she was seeing. I don't remember going for the propofol. I was fighting it as hard as I could. We sorted out the smuggling ring with Haley's murder and investigated Doctor Wheeler and there are no suspects. If we apply Occam's razor, we..." I couldn't continue.

She walked up to me, took my hand in her little hands, her green eyes wide and compassionate.

"Occam was a dick." She said it seriously without a trace of humor, her face close to full pout configuration.

I just waited, quite sure she wasn't trying to be funny, but not sure where she was going.

"The law of parsimony," she said, stating the more formal name of Occam's razor, "states that simpler solutions are more likely to be correct than complex ones. *More likely,* Walter."

I nodded weakly and she squeezed my hand. It was that super-weak ghostly touch, but I appreciated it. It helped.

She pulled me into a hug, her little body at the right height with me still sitting down. The hug almost made it worse. I wanted to cry. I wanted to rage at myself. I had been so stupid to use propofol in the first place, to keep it in the office, to not go get help for that particular addiction.

When she stepped back, her nose was wrinkled and she said, "You stink, Walter."

"What?" I was completely confused. Ghosts don't have a sense of smell so she couldn't possibly be smelling me.

"You stink bad." Her whole face scrunched up like she was smelling something terrible.

"Emily… I…?"

"You stink of murder," her eyes widened with a lust no four-year old could ever experience.

"Emily. Please… I…" I mumbled. I was teetering already, and this tact wasn't really helping. Was she trying to be funny?

"I'm serious, Walter. Which is the simplest explanation? That my murder sense is off for once or that you fell off the wagon? So it wasn't a peachy day, but it wasn't *that* bad of a day."

"I… you know, Emily, addictions are complicated. It's possible that it could have happened."

She nodded slowly. "But not probable. It's also not probable that my first impression of you was wrong. You stank of murder then and you stink of murder now."

I just sat there, my mind reeling. I thought it was brave of me to open up to the possibility of an overdose, but to have it so vehemently resisted, I didn't know what to say or what to do.

"So that was your last day," she said, crossing her arms. "You haunted the practice and Midge for—what? —months."

I nodded.

"So tell me about that," she continued. "There's a clue there. Something you haven't remembered. I know it."

Part Two

DEAD

Chapter Nine

FIRST OF ALL, I KNOW, DEATH BY PROPOFOL IS NOT A BAD
way to go, the effects of the anesthesia can be quite pleasant. But dead is dead and when propofol is used as a
murder weapon or is the instrument of an accidental overdose, it's not a pleasant thing.

When I "woke up" and saw the needle in my arm, the
elastic band loose around it, my first thought was, "Shit,
Walter. Not this. Not again."

I didn't know I was dead. I was in the Monroe room in
the pale-blue dental chair, the sodium yellow glow of a
Tucson night sneaking in through the window, the office
lights off. I heard the sleepy hum of late-night Tucson
outside and everything was quiet in my office.

My escape from Hollywood post-divorce had not been
easy and I dealt with some serious depression. As I have
explained, I turned to gambling and propofol.

Counseling and antidepressants would have been a
much better choice, but, you know, that would require me
to talk about myself and my past, which is something I'm

getting better at now that I'm a ghost, but I was frankly terrible at as a corporeal being.

Human Self-Expression 101 was not a course they taught in college, and like many humans (looking at the gentlemen readers) I needed not only the 101 course, but the 202 and the 303 and the 404. I mean, I think I'm a decent human being, and I do try my best, but getting out words that even halfway describe how I'm feeling is usually worse than a root canal.

But I got through that, so as I stumbled out of the chair, still not having a single clue as to what had happened, but thinking I had relapsed, I was racking my brain trying to remember, trying to understand why I would do this to myself—not kill myself, I didn't know I was dead yet, but using propofol again.

I was having a perfectly understandable reaction. There was a needle stuck in my pale arm, a vial of milky-white propofol on the instrument table next to the dental chair, the office quiet and the lights off.

This was a scene I had repeated many times, waking up predawn from a blissfully quiet propofol-induced sleep. Waking up that way brought the fog of forgetting with it, and that was part of what I liked about it. Forgetting my failure as an actor, my failure as a husband. Forgetting how I had made it to middle age with a career, plenty of debt, and an epic amount of loneliness, but not much else.

I got up and stumbled out of the Monroe room into the hall and I felt so strange. I wasn't dizzy or anything, but I was oddly numb, like the anesthetic effect of the drug hadn't worn off. My body felt distant, indistinct, like it wasn't my own. But my eyes could see so well in the dark office with the scant light leaking in the windows. Was this some side effect of propofol I hadn't experienced yet? I looked down and the needle wasn't in my arm anymore and I had no memory of removing it. I shrugged and tried to stumble out of the room, but something was stopping me.

I looked right behind me and there was this glowing silver cord snaking back into the room. I had no idea what it was and I was so disoriented I wasn't curious. I just shrugged again and surged forth, meeting more resistance, so I just tried harder.

Not that I was aware of what I was "trying." I mean, I thought I was walking, but that is not what was going on. I didn't have a body and I had no idea about that yet. And didn't know it, but that silver cord was attaching my spirit to my body.

I was in this primal space and rather dumb and just tried to go forward again and heard a loud snapping sound and found myself in the hallway. I was glad to be free of the resistance, but uninterested in what it had been.

I went down the hallway into the supply room. There I blinked and shook my head. Below the picture of Sun and me, the short metal cabinet had been forced open, the grey door bent enough to bypass the cheap lock. The orderly assemblage of items in it looked like it had been hastily rifled through, the other vials of propofol lying on their sides in disarray.

But I didn't break into that cabinet, did I?

Memories of my last day came flooding back. So vivid. Haley. The mystery of Midge wanting to keep Haley. Talking to Sun for the first time in two years. I could remember every detail of the day, the sounds and smells and tastes, such as I had never experienced before.

And the present seemed strange and muted by comparison. Beyond my sensitivity to light, I found that I could hear very well but I couldn't smell. The break room, where I found the jimmied cabinet, didn't smell of stale coffee and microwaved burritos. The office didn't have that anti-septic tang that I, honestly, loved. And while I could see just fine, my hands and arms looked strange. In the dark they seemed to both glow and to be partially transparent. It didn't make sense. As I stood there staring at the picture of Sun and me, I realized I couldn't see my own nose.

Well, none of us actually *sees* our nose, not clearly, but it sits there in between our eyes, our brain often editing it out of what we see. But if you think about it, there's a shadow there in the lower center part of your vision. And your eyebrows and eyelashes, they sometimes impinge too.

I turned my head trying to see where my nose was. I tried to furrow my brow, but my sense of my own body was numb and indistinct, and I couldn't do it in a way that entered my visual field.

And then I tried to blink. Nothing. I tried to close my eyes. Again, nothing. What the hell?

Something was wrong. The propofol had really screwed me up. I panicked.

Well… yes, it was panic I was feeling, but it was more like the idea of panic, lacking the full body, hammering heart, sweating pits experience. It was indistinct too.

And that made the panic I could experience, the mental part, get even worse.

I surged out of the supply room and down the hall and past the treatment rooms. I had to get to a mirror. Turn a light on. See what had happened to me.

At the plain white bathroom door, my hand just went through the silver handle.

What?

I tried again and my hand flowed right through, this time my fingers disappearing into the door.

How screwed up was I?

I tried again, my reach off and my whole hand went through the door and the handle.

I did it over and over, like I was caught in some twisted nightmare. My hand reaching out and passing through the handle, through the door, through the wall as my swings got wider, as I got more desperate.

I heard a whimpering sound and stopped my vain attempts, looking for the source of the noise when I realized it was me doing the whimpering.

That stopped me. I stood there, for how long I can't say, my mind slipping, unable to process what I was experiencing.

I looked down and saw that I didn't have legs, not really. The lower half of my body was a vaguely blue shape that kind of looked like two legs in scrubs at my waist, but then became a diffuse mess around my feet.

I had no nose or eyebrows that I could see. I couldn't blink or close my eyes. My body was glowing and transparent. My feet looked like a dissipating cloud of blue.

A dream. This must be a dream. If I got back to the place this all started, maybe I would wake up.

I slowly turned around and went back down to the Monroe room and looked in.

There slumped on the dental chair was the body of a man with curly black hair and a needle sticking out of his arm. He looked like he was dead.

I screamed.

Chapter Ten

EMILY AND I WERE STANDING IN THE HALL OF WHAT WAS
once Hollywood Dental staring into the first treatment
room. The room where I died.

"I wish I had found you sooner," Emily said quietly.

I nodded. It still wouldn't have been good, but it would
have been better.

The line between life and death is stark. Razor thin. I
bet a lot of ghosts have said something like this as they tell
their stories here at the SECI chamber, that typewriter for
ghosts, but it's true.

I was alive and healthy one moment and then another
moment—how much later, really—I was dead. Was the
line a second? A millisecond. A nanosecond? Less?

How long did it take for the irreversible journey from
alive to dead take? When my diaphragm stopped working
because it was paralyzed by the propofol? When my heart
stopped beating? When my brain died? When my soul, my
ghostly form, separated from my body.

Maybe with old age or disease the line isn't so thin, isn't

so sharp and stark. Your life shrinks as your ability to function goes away until you are in a coma, until your life ends.

No. I don't buy that. The change is still abrupt. Very abrupt. Even if you were like my mother and spent a few days in hospice, slipped into a coma, that line was still sharp. Breathing one moment and not the next.

We stood there, two ghosts silent for a long time. As the light faded from the sky, as the sodium yellow glow of streetlights leaked into the room, as the traffic outside lessoned. As the living went on with their endless biological maintenance.

We were ghosts. Time was different for us.

"I'm sorry, Walter," Emily finally said.

I nodded my head, not understanding what she was sorry for. Maybe that I died. Maybe that she maneuvered me into reliving it all. Maybe for the fact that we all have to die.

I didn't want to know what she was sorry for. "It's okay," I mumbled.

"Can you continue?" she asked.

I thought about it, time slipping away from me again. I wanted to stop. I needed to stop. But I felt something pulling me forward. This wasn't about Emily and her wanting me back and basically forcing me into this. This was about me. About understanding how I got here to be this ghost detective who can't solve his own murder with Emily as a partner.

I had to continue, so I did.

Chapter Eleven

I STARED AT ME, AT THE CORPSE IN THE DENTAL CHAIR, for the longest time. What used to be me.

What I was experiencing was not a dream, but in many ways the way my mind was acting was like it was. Time slipped by, rapidly sometimes and at other times it crawled like molasses. My thought processes were strange and disconnected.

"Wow," I thought. "That guy looks just like me. Poor bastard, he overdosed. I wonder if he meant to do that?"

My excellent vision could see every wrinkle in the slack face of the man in the dental chair who looked just like me. He wasn't old, but he was getting there.

"You dye your hair, don't you?" I said, nodding, noticing the slightest splash of silver at some of his roots.

"Did you mean to overdose?" I asked him. "I guess I should call someone."

And then the needle sticking out of his arm caught my attention. I don't know why, but it seemed wrong for it to just be sticking there, a few drops of blood encrusted around it. "You mind if I take this out?" I asked the dead guy I wasn't accepting was me yet.

"Not very talkative, are you?" Suddenly in my mind the man wasn't dead, just sleeping it off, and I started to feel jealous.

I tried to pull the needle out, but my hand just went through it. "Okay, then, I guess you don't want me to take it out. I guess you don't like to share. Be that way."

I stood there for the longest time staring at the arm and the needle in the arm, and then looking at the vial of propofol on the instrument tray, and I felt like a starving man looking at a steaming plate of food that I couldn't reach.

"Got any other needles, bud? I mean, it looks like there is enough of that stuff to go around." I looked around, afraid someone else might be here, that Mother Midge might have heard, and then she would quit, and that would be me losing yet another person that was important to me, and there would go my practice.

I started moving around the room. What I wanted to do, what I was trying to do, was pace, but that wasn't quite possible with my vaporous legs and nonexistent feet.

I kept glancing at the propofoled guy in the dental chair who looked so damn familiar. I did this for a long time. I don't know how long. Every once in a while, I would stop, try to pull the needle out, ask if I could have some propofol, and then get mad at him and start "pacing."

It was like a weird dream. I was caught in a loop. I couldn't get out of it.

My mind would not accept what I was seeing.

That the person in the chair was me.

That I was dead.

That I was a ghost.

But it wasn't a dream, and the sun came up, and Midge came in to work.

"Walter," she called. "You here, hon? The door was unlocked, but the lights are off. What's going on?"

And then I was there with Midge at the entryway to Hollywood Dental as the lights came on. The waiting room was painted a calming pastel blue and festooned with framed pictures of old Hollywood stars. Greta Garbo in *Mata Hari*, Katherine Hepburn in *Morning Glory*, Humphrey Bogart decked out in his trench coat and fedora from *Casablanca*, and so many more.

She walked to the reception desk, her head swiveling around. "Walter?"

I didn't speak. I don't know why. I just followed Midge, curious. My mind wasn't right yet, I can't say that I was sane. But Midge, I knew her. Mother Midge, she would figure it out.

Worry blossomed on her face as the seconds passed, her furrowed brow making her look older.

From the waiting room, down the hall, you can see just a slice of the Monroe room... and the dental chair... and the body lying in the dental chair.

"You didn't sleep here again, did you, Walter?" she asked, but her voice was hushed, barely above a whisper. I noticed her hand shaking that clutched her brown purse to her chest.

What was she talking about? Why was she speaking so quietly? Was she trying not to wake the man in the chair?

And what was going on with her perfume? I couldn't smell it—and you could always smell Midge's perfume. It was like she took it as her mission to make the world a better smelling place. It was one of those smells I didn't actually like, but I found comforting because I associated it with Midge.

I was about to ask her about it when she swept forward. "Walter!" She was yelling now and running. She screamed my name when she got to the door and dropped her purse. She stood there shaking and huffing like she had just run a race.

"Walter…" she said, but this time quietly, mournfully.

I was so confused. I was standing right here. She had walked right by me.

She walked farther into the room, her steps slow and tentative, like a toddler just finding their feet. I couldn't see her anymore and I moved to the doorway.

There, Midge held two fingers to the neck of the body on the chair. "Oh, Walter," she said, this time with such sadness, I wanted to cry.

So the guy was dead. I guess that made sense, he had been lying there still since I woke up. But why was Midge so sad, and why was she telling me?

"Damn you!" Midge said, suddenly standing up straight. Even though "damn" is a very mild curse, it was an unusual thing for Midge to curse at all. "I shouldn't have agreed to that cabinet. I should have got that goddamn drug out of here. I should have…"

She bunched up like someone had just hit her in the stomach and started crying. Big heaving messy sobs. She fell to the floor and gasped out my name over and over while she cried.

I moved farther into the room and really looked at the body. I could see with just a little light, but now that there was full lighting, I could see everything. The drool dried at the corner of the man's mouth, the vacant look in his slitted eyes, the pale tone of his skin, and his face. I really looked at his face.

Time slipped past me again while I looked at the body's face and it slowly dawned on me that it was *my* face.

And the rest of what had happened suddenly made sense (sort of). My legs, my glowing and translucent arms, my hand going through things, not being able to see my nose.

"Yes, this is Midge Williams at Hollywood Dental on East Broadway. There's been an accident." She wasn't crying anymore, but still on the floor, her cell phone out. "There's been an overdose."

That was me in the dental chair with the needle sticking out of his arm… my arm.

I was looking at my own body, but how?

"His name is Walter Anchor. He…" her voice broke and the sobbing briefly came back. "He is dead."

Chapter Twelve

GUILT IS HEAVY.

It's like tying sandbags to yourself and trying to run a race. It slows you down. It changes your every moment. It slows your steps. It makes it hard to function normally.

Guilt feels so heavy. And there in what was once the Monroe room with Emily I felt like I was loaded down with the sandbags of guilt.

As a ghost, our sense of touch is very limited as is the sense of our ghostly form. We never feel heavy. In fact, there is a lightness that is endemic to being a ghost. It can make it hard to be grounded. It's why we walk and act as human as possible even when we don't have to.

But right then, after telling Emily about the moment I realized that I was a ghost and I was staring at my own corpse, I felt so heavy.

Emily had taken my hand and I hadn't even noticed.

"Maybe I was murdered," I said quietly to the dark room, "but it was my fault."

"What?" Emily asked, sounding surprised, as if she

had been stuck in the dream of my death and was just waking up. "What are you talking about, Walter?"

"The propofol. The addiction. That was me," I said. "If I hadn't kept it in the building then I couldn't have died that way."

I wasn't looking at Emily but staring at the damn dental chair, the place I died. It was the same one, I was sure of it. The wear pattern on the faux leather quite distinct. They hadn't replaced it.

"You were murdered," she said, her voice fierce. "If the propofol wasn't here, they would have found another way."

I turned and looked at her. She had the round face of youth, but it was sour like the old ghost she was. "How can you be sure?" I asked.

"I'm sure," she growled.

I love Emily, but she is not perfect. It's her imperfections that are the most loveable parts of her, really. I nodded, weakly, to acknowledge what she was saying, not to agree with her.

"Keep going, Walter," she said, her voice still half growl.

And I did.

Chapter Thirteen

THE BODY WAS GONE. MY BODY WAS GONE.

I stood there in the Monroe room of Hollywood Dental, my mind whirling. Half the time it was "the" body. The other half it was "my" body.

The ambulance had come and gone.

The police had come and gone.

The words "suicide" and "accidental overdose" were said boldly, clearly, no one hesitating.

Mother Midge sold me out and told them I had had a problem with propofol. That I had had problems with gambling. That I was divorced and depressed and childless. That I had once been an actor.

It was all true, but it sounded like an indictment of me despite her tears and sniffing and blubbering. Like all I was could be summed up as propofol addict, gambler, divorcee, and failed actor.

Like that is what should be etched in granite on my tombstone.

Here lies Walter Anchor. He loved to gamble, take propofol, and tell everyone he met of his small acting victories during the "good ole days" before his more talented wife divorced him.

The office was shut down for the day and I was soon alone, the emptiness and the bright Tucson sun outside making it feel ghostly somehow, abandoned. There should be people here. There should be the whir of drills, the slurp of suction, and the sharp smell of antiseptic.

Instead it was me wandering around, my mind slipping, my regret building, the bardo calling.

As I mentioned, the bardo is a term used around the graveyard for that place the "classic" moaning ghost is trapped. A hell of their own making where they relive their own regret over and over.

Hell indeed.

And oddly, sinking into the bardo is tempting. Just like when you are standing on a high precipice, peering over, and jumping is bizarrely tempting. Or maybe that's just me.

The bardo is a lot like addiction. It whispers into your ear that it is better, far better than what you are currently experiencing. But the bardo, just like addictions, is a damn liar.

And I think I would have fallen off that precipice into the bardo if not for Doctor Wheeler.

The next morning, he came into the office first—let me tell you, that had never happened before—whistling like some damn songbird on the first day of spring.

I'm pretty sure he was whistling "Don't Worry, Be Happy."

And that just made me mad.

And all of those scary ghost movies… the grain of truth in them is that ghosts can be pretty unpleasant when they are mad.

I'm not very good at the whole haunting thing. That

morning, my first morning as a ghost, when Doctor Wheeler came in whistling a happy tune, I attached to him.

I can't explain the mechanism, since I don't really know how it works, but for that day everywhere he went, I went. I was dragged along... everywhere... even to the bathroom where he took way too long on the toilet and poked at his damn phone the whole time.

I watched him wash his hands—he, thankfully, did a good job of that—and then make eye contact with himself in the mirror for far too long. He ended in a sly smile and a nod, and while I couldn't read his thoughts, I'm pretty sure it was some narcissistic egotistical self-promotion. Something like, "You got this, Wheeler!"

I was there with him when Mother Midge came in, her eyes red rimmed, her brown-going-to-grey hair flat and lifeless. I saw him consciously wipe the smile off his face before he rounded the corner and saw her. He held out his arms and she collapsed into his embrace.

"I... I didn't sleep," she said, sniffing. "Not for a minute. Poor Walter. I can't believe he..."

"There, there, Midge," he said, rocking her gently, his blue eyes bright now that she couldn't see him. "I know today is going to be tough. But we've got to get the patients rescheduled. Our hearts are heavy, but this is about them."

She sniffed and nodded her head while it was still buried in his chest.

"I know just what to do, Midge. I know just what to do."

And he did. As if he had thought this through. As if he was the one that put the needle in me and ended my life.

MY FIRST DAY AS A GHOST, IT WAS DOCTOR WHEELER

61

and his easeful transition into leading Hollywood Dental that had my full attention.

I was there as he and Midge worked side-by-side calling patients, telling them the sad news, rescheduling their appointments.

This was the first time Wheeler had picked up the phone to call a patient about scheduling, and yet he seemed to be perfectly comfortable with it.

While Midge was sniffing half the time, taking awkward gulps of air, Wheeler was cool and collected. It would go something like this.

"Yes, he was found dead in the office. No, I cannot comment further until the police have completed their investigation, but I can assure that it was nothing communicable and after the weekend we will be open and ready for patients. No, he didn't really have any family, but the authorities have contacted his ex-wife in LA."

I got close enough to listen to the other side of the conversation, but only at first. They left a lot of innocuous messages, but the spectrum of reactions to those they talked to directly was breathtaking. From "Oh my God, I can't believe it. Dr. Anchor was such a kind man," to "I can't reschedule, I have to get this tooth fixed before my vacation."

And there were business realities too that Wheeler seemed to have a grasp on what to do about. I owned Hollywood Dental, well... most of it anyway. I gave Wheeler a ten percent share as a signing bonus and Midge owned ten percent—an additional inducement to stay the last time one of my addictions got the better of me. But mostly it was the banks that owned it. There was some value in the practice, but not a ton.

My will, which I knew someone would get around to soon, left everything to Sun. But Sun didn't need the money or the hassle and Wheeler knew it. He didn't come out and say it, but I read between the lines as he and Midge talked after all the calls were over. He was going to buy it from her and he would get it for a song.

He placed his hand gently on Midge's, they were still both behind the counter, Midge slouched in exhaustion. "I know that was hard and I am sorry for that, but listen to me, Midge. I know what to do. I will keep the practice going. We will all still have jobs. Just trust me."

Midge looked at him with her tired brown eyes and he held her gaze with a gentle smile and a small nod of his head.

"What... we..." she mumbled. "Do we need a lawyer? Walter owned most of the company."

Wheeler kept nodding slowly. "I already talked to one. I know what to do."

"And... services, we need services, a memorial. Poor Walter." She almost devolved into tears again but sniffed and nodded.

"You will do a brilliant job with that, Midge. I know Walter relied on you for everything, that he would want you to do that."

She nodded slowly.

"And I know good old Walter would want us to soldier on. To keep helping patients too... what did he say to me that morning? He would want us to go on 'saving the world one mouth at a time.'"

He kept talking but I couldn't hear him anymore. I had said that phrase sarcastically, to ward him off. He was telling Midge what I would want, but he hardly knew me.

My world became tinged in red. I wanted to do nothing more than to hurt Doctor Elias Wheeler. To put my hands around his neck and squeeze.

And then it occurred to me that Wheeler had the most

to gain from my death. Here he was sliding right in as if he had been planning it all along.

Things got even redder and my vision started tunneling in.

Wheeler killed me. I just knew it, the propofol having erased my memory of it.

Maybe I wasn't alive anymore, maybe I didn't have hands to wring his neck, maybe I was a ghost, but there must be a way to hurt him.

I put my ghostly hands around his neck and "squeezed" wishing that he was dead, that I was killing him.

His eyes widened and he stopped in mid-sentence and cleared his throat.

I had done it. I had done something, at least.

"Where was I?" he asked Midge.

"You were asking about his will," she said, "whether I had ever met his ex-wife."

He nodded sharply. "Right. So...?"

That was it? I made him clear his throat with all my rage. What the hell?

If I had felt helpless when I was alive, I had been fooling myself. This was much worse.

I just stood there and listened while Wheeler outlined how he would take over my practice.

WHEELER DENTAL.

That was the crowning jewel of Doctor Wheeler's plan. Paint over the murals, take down the Hollywood pictures and rename the practice once he owned it.

Wheeler Dental.

He actually had the insensitive, narcissistic cojones to tell Mother Midge that the day after I had died.

I was apoplectic.

I screamed. I raged. The world went red-tinged. I gripped his throat over and over with my ghost hands and squeezed. I made him clear his throat. I made him cough.

And that was it.

And then he was gone and I was left alone watching Midge quietly cry back behind the counter of what would not much longer be Hollywood Dental.

Part of me was curious that I hadn't followed Wheeler. He had motive. He had opportunity. Maybe he drove past the office after midnight, saw that my car was still there and the lights were off. This was the opportunity he had been waiting for. He took the vial of propofol out of his glove box, put on a headlamp, snuck up, and dosed me before I could wake up. After I had stopped breathing, he jimmied the cabinet and left things looking like I had just overdosed.

"He did it, Midge," I whispered to her. "He killed me. We need to catch him. This is how we make it better."

She couldn't hear me, of course.

And while I believed it, I had no way to prove it and I had no way to tell anyone about it.

And then Midge blew her nose and shut all the lights off. She stood at the door gazing in with a look I can't really describe very well. Her eyes were red-rimmed, her round face was sad, but there were layers of other emotions on her face. Regret, for sure. Guilt, maybe.

"Goodbye, Walter," she whispered.

I stood there for a moment staring at her and then at the empty space where she had been. It was almost as if she knew I was here.

Or she was resigning herself to the fact that Wheeler

would be erasing me out of this place at his first opportunity.

I wanted to follow Midge, to listen to her talk to her husband about me. I wanted to know what was going on with her and Haley. I couldn't do anything here, but I couldn't leave either.

I tried. I floated to the door and couldn't go any farther. I was stuck in Hollywood Dental, which was now officially haunted. By me.

Chapter Fourteen

"THIS IS EXHAUSTING," I TOLD EMILY. WE WERE IN THE
reception area and I had been pacing, telling her of my
time haunting my own dental practice.

She nodded, a grim smile on her face.

I was walking carefully, like Emily had taught me. I was
still back to my default ghostly form of scrubs, but that felt
right somehow. I couldn't be bothered with niceties. I had
all this energy now. All this anger.

Wheeler never cared about me. I was just an opportunity to him. My past was with me so strongly that I could
almost hear them talking. I could remember what it was
like being a new clueless ghost. I felt so useless, so power-
less, so confused.

"Do you need a break, Walter?" she asked quietly.

"No," I snapped and kept walking. "I need to get
through this. I need to be done with this."

Emily backed up a step into one of the armchairs. A
very unusual faux pas for her. A dim part of me felt bad for
scaring her, but this was her fault. She had started all of
this. She had made me do this. Did she expect me to feel

nothing, to just stumble onto the clue we had missed so we could happily go solve my own murder and get back to normal?

But we're dead, what the hell is normal anyway?

Is it normal to be a ghost? To be a ghost that solves murders? To be a ghost that types up our cases so justice can be served?

As I write this, I have a little more clarity on what was going on with me. I was getting close. I was almost there. Part of my mind knew what was coming, knew that it would be bad. And that energy was spilling out in unhealthy ways.

Emily set her jaw and stepped out of the chair. Her face was a stern mask that didn't match with her apparent age. "Then get on with it, Walter," she growled.

Chapter Fifteen

WHILE HAUNTING HOLLYWOOD DENTAL IN ITS FINAL days under that name, I learned a lot about people. I had nothing else to do but to follow and listen. All day. Every day.

I couldn't leave the practice, and every morning when someone came in, I was so glad for something else to do but to stew in my own regrets and wander the empty offices staring at the pictures of Hollywood icons and my brief life working there.

And let me tell you, on a Monday morning when someone came in after being a ghost alone in the offices all weekend, I didn't leave their side. Not for a moment. So starved I was for something, anything.

So I learned things.

Haley had a horrible habit of chewing her fingernails and she would sometimes be obsessive with running her fingers through her long brown hair, as if she were a Victorian lady with a prescription for how many times to brush her hair at night.

Wheeler had IBS or—and this would be much worse—

just liked to take breaks, long breaks, while sitting on the toilet fiddling with his phone. Lacking a sense of smell, it was hard for me to tell which. He was also the aforementioned narcissist, and while he was good at manipulating people, he couldn't even do simple math in his head.

Mary Paulson, once she got back from her maternity leave, had a terrible case of postpartum depression and would sneak into the bathroom and flick through the live streams of the cameras she had set up in her own home to see her baby and the woman she had hired to care for him. She seemed tired, strung out, and more than a little bit distracted.

Mary was about ten years older and a lot stouter than Haley and really disliked the younger woman. Haley was supposed to be gone, but she wasn't. Midge and Wheeler had kept her.

Midge was hiding desperate insecurities under her mother hen personality. I often caught her whispering affirmations to herself. "You can do this, Margaret." "You are strong and capable." "You make a difference."

She also had debt problems and was being hounded by creditors.

And on it went for each employee of the office, and even those that worked for the cleaning service that came in at night. I watched. I listened. I learned.

I was trapped there for months and had nothing else to do.

I didn't know it then, of course, but this was the training ground for becoming a ghost detective. Because watching and listening are our main tools.

And I slowly started to see patterns. There was something linking Wheeler and Haley and Midge. They passed packages around and spoke cryptically about them.

About three weeks into my haunting, Midge handed a

package to Haley and said, "You'll get this delivered today."

It wasn't a question. It was the end of the day, Haley out of her scrubs and into jeans and a pink blouse, Midge behind the counter, rising briefly to hand the package over and then going back to the computer.

It was out of the blue. No context whatsoever. The manila envelope plain but with a sticky note on it with an address.

Haley nodded, studied the address and then crunched it up and put it in the recycling bin.

And that was it.

Something was going on.

I tried to follow Haley, but just couldn't leave. It's not like there was a barrier or anything, I just couldn't do it. I would get to the door and couldn't go any farther.

And while I wouldn't solve the mystery of that package, not until I was with Emily and investigating Haley's murder, it did change something in me.

First there was a brush with cynicism. Seeing people more clearly, seeing them vulnerable (which happened a lot more than I thought), seeing their weakness and foibles and how everyone was looking out for themselves made me like them a lot less, made the world a darker place for a while.

But then I watched more. Midge used those affirmations so she could hold the rest of the practice up. She was building up everyone all the time and no one was doing it for her, so she had to do it for herself.

I felt so bad about that.

And then I started seeing how everyone in that office, to a person, was struggling on one level or another. I mean, I knew I was a mess most of the time, but somehow my ego hadn't let it dawn on me that *everyone* was a mess most of the time.

And they were all grieving on one level or another.

Wheeler, although he was eager for the reins of the practice, found it to be very overwhelming. The buck was stopping with him and that meant so many mind-numbing decisions, from raises, to how to discipline late employees, to questions of taxes and what vendors to use. His usually bright face started to sag after a few weeks of this.

Haley was moody and I got to see bright flashes of anger.

"You okay?" Mary asked Haley one day. Haley was in the break room, her shoulders hunched, sipping on coffee and staring at the picture of Sun and me still hanging on the wall. The old grey metal cabinet had been replaced with a new black one. It still held the propofol and I still wanted it.

Mary was a big-boned blond with round cheeks and kind brown eyes.

Haley nodded. "I miss him," she said quietly.

Mary looked around, and seeing that they were alone, said, "It's not the same here without him. I can't stand it that they are going to change the name, take all his pictures down."

Haley turned, her eyes wide. "Not this one, I hope."

Mary shook her head and smiled ruefully. "Not while Midge works here."

I was glad to see the two of them getting along, having something of a conversation. And then silence descended as they both stared at that happy picture of Sun and me.

And then Mary sniffed, turned away, her shoulders gently shaking.

"I know," Haley said, taking Mary into her arms. "I miss him too. It's… I don't…"

And then they were both crying.

I almost didn't stay. I honestly can't tell you which is

worse. Watching people grieve for you or watching people who don't seem to care at all that you are gone.

But something drew me close and I floated over and heard the women whispering.

"Doctor Wheeler is..." Haley began. "I don't..."

Mary nodded and squeezed her. "He didn't... did he?"

My nonexistent heart seized up. How had I not seen it, that the lovely young Haley was just the type that Wheeler always seemed to be dating. Which always puzzled me how the stocky, head-shaven older man got all these younger women.

Haley pushed away for a moment, smoldering anger in her eyes. She shook her head. "Let him try something. I'll..." and then her shoulders slumped and the anger bled out of her and she was holding Mary again. "No. It's just... I miss Walter."

Mary nodded and I could see her face. Tears flowed freely out of her brown eyes and she bit her lip before saying, "I know. I do too. Walter... he was special. He was..." Wracking sobs took hold of her and I would have left if I could. I felt like I should. Like this intimacy was something I shouldn't be watching, but it was about me.

After the crying subsided, Haley whispered right in Mary's ear, so low that no one else but a ghost could hear. "Did you... did you love him?"

My mind raced as Mary took a big shuddering breath and nodded her head slowly.

Mary who had just had a baby. Mary who had been my assistant since the beginning. She was my first hire, even before Midge. She had been by my side for years. Had been my friend. Had talked to me about her struggling marriage and how she hoped the surprise pregnancy would bring them together. I felt genuine affection for her, but I had never imagined that...

"Oh, shit," Wheeler said, strolling into the room, his head shaking. "Let me guess. The Walter Anchor Fan Club is in session."

The women fled. Wheeler pulled something from the supply cabinet and left. But I stayed there, my mind reeling. How could I not have known?

PATIENCE IS A GHOST'S BEST FRIEND. SOMETIMES YOUR only friend. The patience to stay with someone until you get the clue you need to break the case. The patience to continue haunting your old practice until something changes and you can leave. The patience to get through the lonely times where there is literally nothing to do until you get to your next spectral interaction.

I think that my failures in life, my addictions and attempted recovery from them, prepared me for my afterlife.

The bardo, while tempting, never took me. It came calling every day I haunted the office, most strongly at night when I was alone, but I knew addictions and I knew what they felt like, and the bardo felt like the worst kind of addiction. One that promises everything and delivers nothing.

But knowing that Mary... that she...

I can't even type it yet. Let me rephrase.

Knowing how Mary felt, that I had missed it, completely. That if I had known how she felt I might have made different choices... I might have...

Well, let me continue being honest. Mary wasn't my type. And I say that in the most shame-filled way I can. She was a big woman of Germanic descent, while my ex-wife was a slim Hollywood actress of Korean descent.

Mary could never live up to Sun in my mind. I'm sure she knew it. I'm sure this is why she never made her feelings clear.

But what drove me to consider the siren's call of the bardo, as I stood in the supply room/break room during one of the last days of Hollywood Dental, was wondering what if I had known.

What if Mary had poured her heart out to me, confessed her feelings, and I had very gently told her that I did love her, but as a friend and as a trusted peer.

That wouldn't have been good for her, but it would have been good for my delicate, Hollywood-trained, very human ego. My life might have been different, my life might have been better knowing that I was still lovable. Maybe, if she had done it soon enough, I might never have tried the propofol in the first place.

And even though I had never heard the term bardo yet, didn't quite know what the whispered call that promised escape from all of this was, in that break room, after Mary had told Haley that she had loved me, as the activity of the office swirled around me, I finally gave in.

The call of the bardo was the call of the propofol or of the green felt of the poker table. It promised to take me away from this, from knowing this small thing that could have made a huge difference in my life. If I had known this small thing, I would still be alive.

It wasn't a question in my mind. I "knew" it.

The room started to fade as I started to fall. This was the one thing I couldn't stand. Mary, my sweet, hardworking friend Mary had... she had loved me. And I, a man who was sure he was unloved and unlovable, had missed it.

I would have fallen, then. I would have become one of

those clichéd moaning ghosts and forever haunted the practice, or worse yet, Mary, but Midge saved me.

She was closing up the office and stopped in the break room and stood right in front of me staring at the picture. Midge was short and I could see over her, and her attention caught my attention, the tendrils of it that were still left.

"Okay, Walter. We're done for the day here," she said it quickly and turned to go, but then her shoulders slumped and she turned back to the picture. She sighed, it was long and full of pain. "If I could leave, if I could quit this damn job, I would. It's just not the same without you. I miss you, hon. See you on Monday."

Of course Midge wasn't for the transformation to "Wheeler Dental." Of course she hated it. I had been in my head too much and convinced myself otherwise.

Even though the bardo was still there, still calling, even though it started to whisper to me in Sun's voice saying, "I'm here, Walter. I am waiting for you," I followed Midge.

I didn't think about it when we reached the door and I floated right through it after her. I didn't think about getting in her blue Prius but was suddenly sitting in the passenger's seat beside her.

Midge missed me. Midge must have known how Mary felt.

Thoughts of my murder were gone and I was no longer haunting the practice but haunting Midge.

Chapter Sixteen

EMILY WAS STARING AT ME. MY ANGER HAD BEEN replaced by surprise. I had forgotten about this exchange. I had forgotten that Mary loved me. I had wanted to forget it again.

So even with the clarity of my ghostly memory, I had managed to shove it down, to let it go, to forget it. Until Emily dragged me here and made me walk through it step by step.

And I hadn't told Emily. What I just wrote was all of it, but the version I told Emily I had edited slightly. In it the girls had grieved for me, but Haley hadn't asked Mary if she loved me. I hadn't almost fallen into the bardo before attaching to Midge.

I didn't mean to lie.

It just came out that way.

But I couldn't tell her. I couldn't speak it. I couldn't let that possibility become any more real. The possibility that Mary had been involved in my death.

See... I still can't go there. Mary with her strained

marriage and her post-partum depression. Maybe she had killed me to…

That's where it gets tricky. Yes, Mary had served in the military and had more medical training then a normal dental assistant. Yes, Mary knew all about my propofol problem and would have known how to deliver an overdose.

But… I couldn't imagine it. I couldn't accept it. I still can't.

Then, my mind went to her husband. A big man and also a former soldier. A violent man who had hit Mary. Maybe he did it. Maybe he knew of Mary's feelings and was jealous.

"What's going on, Walter?" Emily asked quietly, a strange look on her face, her lollipop the palest of yellows. She was worried.

We were in the storage room and I was pacing—well, more floating—not even very aware of it. My ghostly form was diffuse, not as bad as when I was a new ghost, but not normal for me anymore.

I focused on it, took some deep breaths, and tightened it up like Emily had taught me.

"It… it was hard to see them cry like that," I said.

Emily's eyes narrowed and the lollipop on her T-shirt snapped back to a cheerful red. She knew I was keeping something from her and had decided to hide her feelings from me. "I bet it was," she said slowly.

I felt a distance between us, one that felt decidedly dangerous. My afterlife worked only because of Emily. But I couldn't tell her about Mary. I couldn't think about her being involved. About her betraying me.

"I… I just need to finish this," I said.

Emily nodded warily and I continued.

Chapter Seventeen

I HAD BEEN TO MIDGE'S HOUSE OVER THE YEARS. AN old, squat house made out of cinder blocks. A plain rectangle with a garage on one end painted a cheery blue. A simple house with a roomy backyard surrounded by other old cinder-block houses in an older Tucson neighborhood.

I had been there for Thanksgiving and Christmas Eve dinners. I had been there for Fourth of July barbecues. I had been there after Hal's heart attack helping out.

I say all of this to make it clear that I knew Midge and her house. I had been there many times. But when she got home, pulled her Prius into the driveway, I was shocked.

The yard was unkempt, far past the need for mowing. The blue paint was starting to peel off the facia and the Christmas lights were still up all these months later.

"What's going on, Midge?" I asked from the passenger's seat. I didn't expect her to hear me. I spoke out of reflex.

Midge was just sitting there, staring at the garage door,

blinking too much, her chin quivering like she was barely able to hold back the tears.

I saw a motion out of the corner of my eye and turned. A young woman was rollerblading over the faded black of the road. She caught my eye and waved at me.

And then I noticed she was a little bit transparent, which was puzzling. A pickup came up from behind her and she didn't notice. I shouted and the truck ran her over and…

No. She was still there. She waved again and skated off.

It took a minute for my mind to engage and realize what I had just seen. She was like me. She was a ghost.

Of course there were other ghosts, I just hadn't seen them since I had spent my entire time dead in my office.

As I wound back our drive in my mind, I remembered seeing way more people at the park we drove by than I expected, considering the heat out there this time of year. Some of them had looked odd. A bit transparent. Maybe floating.

I didn't have time to ponder it because Midge was out of the car and heading towards the house. "You've got this, Margaret," she muttered. "You can handle this."

As she opened the door, I was wishing I was still at the office. As I haunted the place, I got to know its inhabitants in a different way. Was I ready to do that with Midge in her own home?

But it wasn't like I had a choice. I floated in with her and…

Well, nothing really. Midge put her keys in a blue ceramic bowl on a narrow table in the entryway, kicked her shoes off, and said, "Hal. I'm home."

The house looked the same. It was neat and clean with shades of blue dominating. The powder-blue shag carpet was way past the need for replacing, but it had been that way as long as I could remember.

"Honey," Midge called. "How was your day?"

I could hear the muffled sound of metal clanging and a soft curse. "He's in the garage," I said.

Midge walked through the small two-bedroom house and then went to the garage where Hal had the hood up on an old Chevy pickup truck. "How was your day, dear?" she asked.

Hal had buzzed-cut grey hair that had receded a good long way from his forehead. He had a barrel chest and thick arms, a faded tattoo of a hula girl on his forearm that he got in the Navy and Midge hated.

"Too damn hot," Hal growled. "Got the McLaren's deck finished, but the truck sounds funny."

Hal was a contractor. After his heart attack he had scaled back and started taking smaller, simpler jobs.

"Dinner's at six," Midge said cheerfully. "And we're supposed to Skype with Rachel tonight."

Hal grunted his ascent and Midge went into the kitchen and started making meatloaf. Rachel is their daughter, a lovely young woman getting her master's in psychology in California.

I felt strange being away from the office. I worried about the other ghosts, like a puppy seeing a big dog for the first time. There had to be more. What would happen the first time I came face to face with another ghost?

Midge cooked and their evening wound down and I began to relax. I hadn't seen any other ghosts. The house needed some maintenance, but nothing horrible was going on here. I watched their call with Rachel. I enjoyed watching TV with them, an episode of one of the many *Law and Order* shows. Normally TV shows other than Sun's weren't my thing, but after being stuck in my head (this is pretty much the literal state of a ghost) for so long, I was happy to be entertained.

And then Hal went to bed.

And then Midge changed.

"It's okay, Margaret," she said, her hands clasped as she rocked in the living room's rocking chair. "We'll find a way. We always find a way."

I had found it odd that she had stayed in her scrubs all evening. Well, not that odd. I had often done it, but I had always thought I was the only one. Scrubs were comfortable. In many ways they were a piece of my post-actor identity. And that piece of identity was important.

After Hal went to bed, I found out why Midge stayed in her scrubs. And it was odd.

Midge had five one-hundred-dollar bills tucked into her bra, like some high-price stripper. Except Midge was short and round and over fifty.

She pulled them from their hiding place with gritted teeth and a long sigh. She went deep into the cabinet under the right-angle bend of her kitchen counter and pulled out a metal lockbox. It wasn't locked, but I can't imagine this was an area that Hal explored. She put the five hundred-dollar bills with a growing stack of money.

"This is the way, Margaret," she whispered. "I know you hate it, but this is the only way."

That night, while Mother Midge slept, I just watched and thought and pondered.

———

HAUNTING MIDGE WAS BORING FOR THE MOST PART.

Midge worked. Midge came home. Midge passed strange envelopes to Haley that she got on her breaks when she walked in a nearby park.

Midge would go and sit awkwardly on a bench, trying desperately to look casual, she just looked ridiculous, her hands roaming around strangely as if she didn't know what to do with them. The woman was not built to be a spy. She would grab an envelope taped to the underside of the park bench and rush away. In the envelope would be money, a sticky note with an address, and another envelope that never got opened. This is where Midge got the hundred-dollar bills. Midge put them in the lockbox after Hal went to bed. Midge worried and talked to herself a lot.

Wheeler was involved with it too. Sometimes he would come back with the envelope and hand it off to Midge. Sometimes Midge delivered the envelopes herself after work. Sometimes she handed the envelope off to Wheeler or Haley.

Whoever got it didn't deliver it, and they never really talked about it. It was just a handoff. Wheeler and Midge kept the cash, Haley got to pad her timecard.

I was there with Midge for every moment of every day, and while it was apparent something strange was going on, I didn't know what it was.

Was this why I was killed?

Had I ever really known Midge? Had I ever really known anyone?

After weeks of this, I don't really know how long it was, I was a wispy mess floating after Midge as she got up, as she took a shower, every time she went to the bathroom, to the office, her feet pounding across the carpeted floors, back home, making dinner, watching TV.

I remember her gathering all those hundred-dollar bills one night after Hal went to bed. She went to the little rolltop desk they had in the living room, got an envelope out, and counted all the money and added it up. She then took a stack of unpaid bills, including overdue mortgage statements, and added those up.

Sweat beaded on her forehead and her round face flushed red.

It was over twenty thousand dollars and I had to wonder how long they had been at this. Right under my nose.

Hal wasn't making the money he used to before the heart attack. Their bills had stacked up. Hal's medical bills. Rachel's college. And all the normal stuff. Midge managed the household funds and hadn't told him how bad it was.

"You did it, Margaret," she said with a satisfied nod. "You did it."

She stuffed all of it into her purse and in the morning, which was a Friday when the office was closed, she took it to the bank. She had cashier's checks made out in the amount of all her bills. She took them to the post office and filled out all the paperwork to send them registered mail. Her hands trembling as she filled out form after form.

"No more," she said when she got back to her car and started it, turning the air conditioner on high, the breeze it created playing with her shoulder-length brown and grey hair. "No more."

And then it was over. Or, at least it seemed to be.

Midge was lighter, happier, but the drone of her days as I was dragged along after her became so dull. Preparing and eating food and eliminating food. Taking care of the house and laundry. Work and shopping. A brief bit of TV in the evening with her husband. Days off where Midge was just as busy, but in the house instead of the office, her feet pounding over those carpeted floors.

Soon I started to filter it all out. I could make no sense of it. The packages. The money. All three of them delivering them. If I had been able to follow Haley, maybe I would have figured something out. But now that it was all over, there were no more clues.

I saw Doctor Wheeler, of course. He was happy. He was cheerful. His plans to take over my office taking shape. He was dating women far too young for him and going through them rapidly.

Every once in a while, I got up the energy to try to hurt him, wrapping my ghostly hands around his throat, but all I ever did was make him cough.

I was a decidedly inept ghost.

And then I just gave up and started filtering it all out. And the more I filtered out reality, the wispier I became. It was hard to tell that I was wearing scrubs anymore, my look edging towards that of a classic ghost, made of nothing more substantial than smoke.

I wasn't thinking about my murder. I wasn't pondering the mystery of Midge and the money. I could hear the bardo calling, promising me relief from all of this, but I didn't believe it. I wasn't quite here and I wasn't quite gone. Not yet.

It's not like you become a ghost and get it all figured out in a day. It's not like you tend to figure it out at all without some help. It's a bizarre experience. The bardo, filled with all your regrets, is waiting and much more tantalizing than facing the reality of your life and addressing your unfinished business. Or even more banal than that, the bardo is much more tantalizing than the boredom of watching the living and the endless treadmill they are on taking care of their biology.

Except as a new ghost you don't even know that you have unfinished business. You just don't know anything.

Without help, without a guide or a mentor, most ghosts fall into the bardo.

And I would have, but for the letter and Emily.

Midge found it in her mailbox one day. A plain white envelope with her address shakily written on it in blue.

She stood there in the heat blinking and staring at it like it was something dangerous.

There was no return address on the envelope.

There was no stamp.

Sweat formed at her hairline and her face flushed red. She grabbed it and shoved it under her scrubs and under her bra strap.

"Just breathe, Margaret," she whispered to herself. "Just breathe. You can do this."

Her use of affirmations had stopped after she got all her bills paid, so this woke me up a bit and I started paying attention.

She walked into the house and said a brief hello to Hal and her daughter Rachel who was visiting from school. They both stared at her as she whizzed by. This wasn't the kind of greeting they were used to.

She went to the bathroom, locked the door, and sat down on the toilet.

She opened the envelope with shaking hands. Inside on a plain white piece of paper written in blue in the same shaking script it said, "If you need to reach me again about your financial problems, drop a note at this address."

It was followed by an address that I knew was in a sketchy neighborhood.

Suddenly I wasn't so disengaged. I wasn't so gone. Here was something real. A clue. An address. A way to find out what all of the passing of envelopes and money with her and Haley and Wheeler was about. Maybe a way to find out who killed me.

Midge's hands shook as she slowly tore up the letter and flushed it down the toilet.

There was fear on her face, but guilt too. I felt a flash of anger, but I understood that circumstances had driven her to this, had made her do whatever it was she had been doing.

She was taking care of her household and her husband and her daughter.

Midge hiked down her scrub bottoms and went to the bathroom for real, her whole body still shaking.

My mind reeled. There was a lot of money here. Was this why I was killed? Was it because of what Midge and Haley and Wheeler were doing? Midge who was someone important to me. Midge who I loved and trusted. Midge who had done so much to make my life here as a dentist work as well as it had.

Had Midge done this to me? For money? So she could pay off her bills and keep her kid in college?

The empathy I had felt twisted back to anger and that twisted into a crushing depression.

I had failed as an actor. I had failed as a husband. I had failed as a dentist. What did any of this matter? My life had been a flop, who cares who killed me?

And then the bardo got loud and I was ready to be away from all this. I was ready to fall into the arms of addiction, to never come back.

The room faded and I could hear Sun laughing. I could see the scrubby hills outside of LA where that happy picture of Sun and I was taken, the one that hung in the storeroom of my dental practice.

"Come on, Walter," I could hear her saying, her voice distant but getting clearer. "Stop with the kissing. It's time to take a picture."

"But I like kissing you," I heard a distant me say. "It's all I want to do."

I knew it was a bait-and-switch, hearing those happy

voices. I knew it wasn't real. That it wouldn't last. I knew this thing was a worse deal than the propofol, but I just didn't care. I just needed to escape.

I was still in the bathroom aware of Midge shaking on the toilet, but I could also see the sun hanging in the clear blue sky above me, and I could smell the dry dust the breeze was kicking up at that shoot. The day was becoming real.

But then I heard another voice. A girl's voice. A little girl. She said, "Not cool, let the lady go to the bathroom in private. What kind of sicko are you?"

And then I wasn't in Southern California anymore and there was another person in the bathroom with Midge and me.

She was short, looking to be about four years old. She wore blue shorts and a white T-shirt with a large red lollipop printed on it. She had blond hair cascading around her round face in ringlets looking very much like Shirley Temple when she was a child actor back in the thirties.

I opened my mouth to speak and did a double take. Her feet weren't quite touching the ground and she was just a little bit transparent. She was a ghost but more substantial than any ghost I had seen. My mouth moved, but I couldn't speak. Sun's laughter faded from my consciousness and I missed it so much.

The little girl ghost put her balled up hands on her hips and said, "You heard me. Leave the lady alone. I mean it."

"I… What…?" I said, finally finding my voice.

"Christ on a stick, are you a bardo-brained perv or what?" she asked.

"Huh?" I said, not understanding what she was talking about. While I had been experiencing the bardo, I didn't have a word for it, much less any idea what "bardo-brained" might mean.

"Did you die in here?" she asked, her voice getting loud like I was hard of hearing. "Are you going to spend the rest of eternity haunting people trying to relieve themselves?"

"No," I said, coming more into myself. "Of course not. I… I was murdered. She knows something, that letter she just read is a clue."

"Well then prove it," she said, turned on her heel, and walked through the bathroom door.

Something made me follow her. Part of it was that she was a different kind of a ghost, part of it was how articulate she was and how young she looked. She spoke with a bit of a lisp making her sound young, but her words were anything but.

I followed her into Midge's living room with its faded blue carpet and preponderance of blue knickknacks.

The girl squared her shoulders and turned to face me. "So, are you trying to be a gumshoe or something?"

I blinked. Not that it did me any good since I didn't have real eyes. I knew she was asking if I was a detective, the archaic slang adding to the mystery of her. "I just want to find out who killed me."

"And then what?" she asked, crossing her arms.

"I… well…" I hadn't thought that far.

She shook her head slowly, giving me a most disapproving look. "You don't know anything, do you?" She looked up and added, "Lord, why me? This fellow is so wet behind the ears he's about to drown." She sighed and looked back at me. "Come along. I guess you've won the lottery, big boy, because ole Emily here is going to show you the ropes."

"I need to stay here," I said. "I need to follow Midge. I need to find out who killed me."

She sighed again. "One-track mind. Can't say I mind that in a man, as long as the track his mind is on is one I like." She gave me a leering grin that was completely out of place on her young face with that lispy voice. "Look... What's your name?"

"Walter."

"Look, Walter. You stay here you will end up in the bardo, a lost cause, a waste of an afterlife. But if you really want to find your killer, come with me now. I'll teach you enough so you can be a proper ghost." With that she walked away from me, to the front door, and right through it.

Down the hall I heard the toilet flushing and then water running. Midge would be coming out. It might be interesting to find out how she acted toward her family.

But the girl ghost who didn't act like a girl said she would teach me. If I knew what the hell was going on, it might help. It might lead to my murderer.

I saw Midge come out of the bathroom and straighten her scrubs. Her lips were moving and I could hear her mumbled affirmations. "You did your best, Margaret. You did what you had to do. For Rachel. For Hal. No one got hurt. It's just another evening. You got this."

I could remember the address from the letter. I could go there any time. I didn't need Midge for that. She had paid off her bills and all the passing of envelopes had stopped at the office.

And then I heard Sun laughing again and could smell the dusty air and feel the sun from that long-ago shoot. The bardo was taunting me, tantalizing me.

But what I wanted wasn't here with Midge or back in the past with Sun. What I wanted was to go to that address and find out who killed me. What I needed was some help in figuring out this ghost thing.

The choice was clear, but it wasn't easy. I stood there, the moments ticking by until I had to move or else Midge would have walked right through me.

I took one step forward and then the next followed and I was outside the front door.

The little girl ghost was there, a wicked grin on her round face that was so out of sync with her apparent age. "Good choice, boy-o," she said. "My name is Emily and I died in 1931 of dysentery." She thrust out her hand.

I looked at it. I was a ghost. How could I shake hands?

"Come on," she said. "I don't bite... at least not that often. Take my hand, tell me your name and how you died."

"What...?" I asked.

"Death 101," Emily said. "You greet a new ghost by telling them your name and how you died. It's just good manners."

I nodded slowly, still trying to figure out how to actually shake hands.

"Come on..."

I put my hand in hers and... I felt something. The barest sense of touch as our hands joined. It surprised me, but in a good way. I had existed for all this time with just two senses, sight and sound, so touch was something of a revelation.

"My name is..." she prompted with a nod.

"My name is Walter Anchor and someone killed me by overdosing me with propofol and I'm going to find them."

She smiled. "Okay, okay. A bit more than asked for, but that was good." She let go of my hand and looked me up and down. "You may not be the brightest bulb but at least you're easy on the eyes."

My jaw hung there as I tried to process a four-year-old looking at me like she had just looked at me and with the lisp it sounded like "eathy on the eyeth." But then I remembered she said she had died in 1931 making her eighty years as a ghost. I could tell that this was going to be interesting.

"Can we go to that address?" I asked. "And look for clues?"

Emily narrowed her green eyes and looked at me closely. She leaned toward me and sniffed loudly. "Yeah... yeah... I can smell it. You were murdered, weren't you?"

"You can smell?" I asked. Probably not the most important question given what she had said, but I really missed smelling.

Her smooth brow furrowed. "Not literally, genius. I just have a sense about these things. And you..." She sniffed loudly again. "...something strange happened to you."

"Yeah," I said. "Someone stuck a goddamn needle in my arm and overdosed me."

"Language, young man!" she said, her eyes wide, stepping back from me and crossing her arms. "You will watch that language around me."

I was beginning to second-guess this decision. I mean, this strange little ghost clearly knew what she was doing, but maybe she was just too strange.

"Umm... sorry," I said.

She sighed. "Well, we best get you to the graveyard and start getting you a little less wet behind the ears."

"And then we'll go to the address?" I asked.

She nodded slowly. "Yes, mister one-track mind, we'll go to the address once you know how to be a ghost. But keep your panties on, it's going to take some time."

I looked back to Midge's plain cinder-block house with the peeling paint. I could hear the drone of the TV from inside as dusk deepened and the lights of the neighborhood flickered on.

My chest hurt and I looked down. My blue scrubs were clearly visible and I wasn't so wispy anymore. Why did my chest hurt? Maybe because since the moment I died I had been connected to the life I had been living. As a dentist at Hollywood Dental working with Midge and Haley and Mary and even Dr. Wheeler.

Emily, the little girl ghost who had been dead for decades was walking away, not looking back, but she was walking slowly. She was a complete unknown, but at least offered some hope for figuring out what happened to me, finding out who killed me.

I was so myopic then. I was a clueless new ghost. I wanted to find my murderer and then... I couldn't even conceive of something more than that. Emily was right, I did have a one-track mind.

Emily was halfway down the street and I still stood there looking back at the house, back at the past, and then looking toward the diminutive ghost and towards the future.

I chose the future.

"Wait!" I yelled and flew to Emily who was still walking.

She gave me a look like she had just eaten something sour. "Walk, Walter. Don't fly."

"What?" I asked. "Why wouldn't I want to fly?

"Just do it," she growled.

So I did. There on Midge's street I tried to walk and... it wasn't easy. I had to think about every single movement. I had no muscles, so there was no muscle memory to guide me.

Emily was patient, slowly coaching me, and in about ten minutes I was doing a fairly scary impression of a human walking. My gait was rather spasmodic, my feet either not touching the pavement or landing inches below, but at least I was walking.

She grinned at me. "Feel better now, don't you?"

I nodded. Because I did. I felt more substantial. I felt more... real. And that one tiny lesson made it clear that I had no clue as to how to be a ghost.

As the night deepened, we kept walking, winding our way through quiet Tucson neighborhoods avoiding the living. My mind cleared and it felt kind of like a meditation.

"I've been thinking," Emily finally said.

I stopped and looked at her. Her mouth was slightly open and she looked like a kid anticipating Christmas morning and all the presents under the tree.

"I can sense murder, right?" she said. "It's how I found you in the bathroom watching that poor woman."

I nodded for her to continue. I really didn't want to talk about that part.

"I find new ghosts that way," she said, "and help them out when I can."

I didn't say anything, the wheels were clearly turning in her mind.

"And you want to be a gumshoe," she said.

"Well... I... I want to solve my own murder," I said slowly.

She nodded. "Yeah. So what if we do both? I find the murders and you solve them. I mean, you've got to learn a lot before we can even try it, but... you know...." her face lit up. "It might be a whole lotta fun."

Her smile was so bright I couldn't tell her that I didn't want to be a detective, that I just wanted to solve my own murder. I was a dentist, and before that an actor. I was not a detective.

But her joy was infectious so I said, "Yeah. That could be fun."

She clapped her hands and hopped up and down, her curls bouncing around her round face. She then got a very serious look on her face, stood up straight, and cleared her throat. "Listen up, everyone," she said to the quiet neighborhood with her lispy voice. "I want to introduce you to Walter Anchor, ghost detective!"

Epilogue

IT WAS DARK ON THE TUCSON STREET NOT FAR FROM Midge's house. As my story had moved, Emily and I had moved. From my old dental office to Midge's house, where everyone was asleep, to the streets of the old neighborhood with one-story cinder-block houses and large mature trees where I first got to know Emily.

The strategy had been effective. The proximity strengthening my already good ghostly memory.

I looked at Emily and she was staring at me, her lollipop still a cheerful red, her face round and youthful, but her expression mature and guarded.

She knew I had left something out.

Something important.

A lead on my cold case.

A clue I couldn't bear to follow.

And she had stopped reflecting her mood through her lollipop T-shirt. She was anything but cheerful.

"You saved me, Emily," I said with my best smile. It's a good smile too, it landed me some parts.

"I am glad, Walter," Emily said with a small nod and a grim tone that did not go with her words.

We were on the section of the street where she taught me to walk. Where she started turning me into a proper ghost. It made the distance between us feel even stranger, because even when we barely knew each other there was less distance.

"I don't know if I ever properly thanked you," I said, keeping up the faux cheerfulness. "I really am so grateful. I would be stuck in the bardo if not for you."

She nodded again and even with her bouncing curls it wasn't a happy thing. "I'm glad I could help you." She tried to smile, but she had too much four-year-old in her and it just looked like she was in pain.

"Look I—" I began.

"I think I—" Emily said at the same time.

"Go ahead," I said with a nod.

"I think I should go, Walter," she said. "I think I'm going to go pop over to Tokyo. It'll be light there. I need to take a walk by the ocean."

I blinked. Same reason you would have—surprise—but it did me no good. Just a stupid biological holdover. I don't have eyes. I can't close them. I had heard that Emily was into travel, and with her popping she could go wherever she wanted. But it was clear that I wasn't invited on this Tokyo stroll.

"Sure. Sure," I said. "Maybe I'll head over to the Midnight Circle. See what play Banquo and the ghosts are putting on."

Emily and I didn't know how to do this. How to talk and not mean what we were saying. How to have a rift between us.

"Sorry I dragged you through all of this," she said with a sheepish grin. "I was just so sure you'd find something."

Her eyebrow arched and it seemed like she was looking into me again, not at me.

She was giving me another chance to tell the truth, a chance to heal the rift before it became serious. I opened my mouth but couldn't find words. My actor's mask of cheerfulness fled me.

And then I felt my face tighten in anger. This was my death. My murder. My case. My secret to keep or to tell. I'm not perfect. I couldn't take this on right now. There was nothing wrong with me taking a step away from it. Giving me time to process it.

"Me too," I said, putting the smile back on my face.

Emily's frown deepened and she took a step down the street away from me.

"But…" I began and she stopped and turned, hope on her round face, her green eyes a little brighter. "I think I'll go to the SECI chamber instead," I continued. "Type all of this up. Maybe by going through it a second time, I'll find something."

Emily looked into me again. She was a skilled enough and wise enough ghost to know that I had found a clue and was just buying time. And she was enough of my friend to let me do that.

"That's a good idea," she said. "You do that. I'll talk to you soon."

With a small smile and a pop she was gone and I was left there alone on the quiet Tucson street wondering if Mary Paulson had killed me. Or her husband. Or both of them.

Or had I slipped after my very bad day and accidently overdosed?

Neither prospect was acceptable. Neither path led anywhere I wanted to go. Being murdered had been so important to my identity as a ghost, but if it had been

Mary, someone I truly cared about, that would further erode my perception of the life I had lived. And if I had done it myself... how was I to "live" with that?

If I tell Emily what I had remembered, we would be off investigating Mary and her husband. If I don't, the rift between us will grow.

Neither of these were acceptable.

I stared down the quiet street, the living sleeping, their porch lights on, their work done for the day. Not thinking about their lives, much less their afterlives.

I had no one to turn to, and without Emily, I felt so alone. I felt pulled west to Hollywood. I could go check on Sun. But what would I find? I could go to a casino and watch the living gamble, hoping that a bit of the old thrill would bleed through. I could go to the Midnight Circle and pretend everything was okay—I was a good enough actor for that, but I had no desire to be around other ghosts.

So I shrugged my shoulders and flew up into the night towards the SECI chamber. To write all of this for you.

What do you think I should do?

Because I still don't know.

More Mystery?

WALTER AND EMILY HAVE A LOT MORE CASES TO SOLVE. Next is "**A Hollywood Kind of Murder**," available July, 2020. Join my email newsletter and never miss a thing.

A Hollywood Kind of Murder

Walter Anchor spends his afterlife solving murders in the hope of one day solving the toughest murder of all. His own.

When a case brings him to Hollywood, Walter takes on a murder that could only happen in Tinseltown. An actor playing the part of a corpse murdered during the filming of a funeral scene. Walter will deal with an interfering ghost and confront his past as a failed actor to

solve this case. But can he stop the murderer before someone else dies?

From the author of *Shuffled Off: A Ghost's Memoir* comes a mystery unlike anything seen before.

Get "A Hollywood Kind of Murder" Now!

About the Author

Robert J. McCarter is the author of seven novels, three novellas, and dozens of short stories. He is a finalist for the *Writers of the Future* contest and his stories have appeared or are forthcoming in *The Saturday Evening Post, Pulphouse Fiction Magazine, Fiction River, Andromeda Spaceways Inflight Magazine,* and numerous anthologies.

His latest effort is a serialized novel called *Woody and June Versus the Apocalypse,* a story of adventure and love and taking things (even the apocalypse) in stride. Of his novel, *Seeing Forever,* Kirkus Reviews says, "Sci-fi as it should be: engaging, moving, and grand in scope."

He lives in the mountains of Arizona with his amazing wife and his ridiculously adorable dogs.

Find out more at:
robertjmccarter.com

Books by Robert J. McCarter

Walter Anchor, Ghost Detective Stories

- **Case 1: Detecting Haley** (also part of *Life After: Stories of Life, Death, and the Places in Between*)
- **Case 2: The Ghost Bride's Gift**
- **Case 3: A Long Hard Fall**
- **Case 4: Death of a Dentist**
- **Case 5: A Hollywood Kind of a Murder** (coming July 2020)
- **Case 6: The Red Arrow Murders** (coming September, 2020)
- **Unfinished Business: The Cases of Walter Anchor Ghost Detective** (coming October, 2020)

For a complete list of Walter Anchor stories, go to RobertJMcCarter.com/WalterAnchor

Novels in the "Ghost's Memoir" world:

- Shuffled Off: A Ghost's Memoir, Book 1
- Drawing the Dead
- To Be a Fool: A Ghost's Memoir, Book 2
- Of Things Not Seen: A Ghost's Memoir, Book 3
- A Boy, a Girl, and a Ghost

For a complete list the "Ghost's Memoir" novels, go to ShuffledOff.com

The Woody and June versus the Apocalypse Series

Find out more at WoodyAndJune.com

The Neutrinoman and Lightningirl Series

Find out more at Neutrinoman.com

Other Novels:

- Seeing Forever

For a more information, go to RobertJMcCarter.com

www.ingramcontent.com/pod-product-compliance
Lightning Source LLC
Chambersburg PA
CBHW030557130626
46552CB00006B/2575